Talks With Dead Aunts

And Other Tales From the Isla Ajaja

by

Carly Berg

Talks with Dead Aunts And Other Tales From the
Isla Ajaja is a work of fiction. Unless otherwise
indicated, all the names, characters, businesses,
places, events and incidents in this book are either the
product of the author's imagination or used in a
fictitious manner. Any resemblance to actual persons,
living or dead, or actual events is purely coincidental

For the captain, with love

Contents

Talks With Dead Aunts

June 1976
The Isla Ajaja, Texas

JACI

    I climb into the back of the old black Cadillac Aunt Verona's so peacock-proud of, just to get a break from her. It's so hot my bare legs stick to the seat. The inside of the car is bright, bright red, which makes it seem even hotter. My mama said it looks like a whorehouse in hell. Aunt Verona takes me getting into the back as a high-level offense against her. She says, "You gonna ride up here with me, Miss Sassy. I ain't your doggone chauffeur."

    I can't stand any more, after whole month of being closely supervised and bossed like I'm five instead of fifteen. I say, "No thank you. I don't require that."

"Excuse me?" she says, pulling her cat-eye sunglasses up on top of her big-wigged head so she can stare me down.

I just can't take no more. I say, "If people see me riding around in this pimpmobile, I'll be ruined."

She opens her eyes real wide, like she is brand new to planet earth and in awe of her surroundings. Then she slaps me.

After that, she gets in front alone and starts driving. I think about opening the car door, to scare her into thinking I'm gonna jump out while the car's moving. Or maybe I'll snatch the wig off her head. The sunglasses, too. Haha! I'd never have the guts, though. Aunt Verona is a big, churchy woman, not the type you'd backtalk, unless you just couldn't take no more of her. My mama don't hardly even talk back to her. We ride along in thorny silence, out of Aunt Verona and Uncle Marty's subdivision, down the highway, then across the bridge over the bay, to the Isla Ajaja. Then we turn right on Beach Drive, on the seawall.

Somewhere over the Gulf of Mexico, a seagull screams like a girl being tortured. I know how it feels. The music ain't on in Aunt Verona's car for once. She probably thinks herself being mad is some big solemn no-music occasion.

Cars are parked in a line on the beach side of the road. Hotels, restaurants and souvenir shops are on the other side, and palm trees are everywhere. The tourists probably don't even know the palms was trucked in from somewhere more tropical, such as southern Florida.

Mama says we're lucky to live where everybody wants to go. She always points out license plates as proof. Aside from all the Texas ones, I see Arkansas, Iowa, Ohio, Louisiana. Sometimes you'll even see a Mexico or Canada plate.

The people on the beach today mostly have the tourist complexion, which is either cottontail pale or sunburned bright pink. "Cottontails" are what they call the new people over at the illegal nude beach. That's what I heard, anyhow.

We BOI (Born on the Island) folks have the sense to stay inside in the air conditioning when it's a zillion degrees out. Or at least in the shade, if there ain't no air conditioner.

It's hotter than hell today, even in a moving car with the windows down.

Dolphins leap up out of the gulf in arcs, like they're showing off for the crowd. On the horizon, a long row of ships wait their turns to enter the ship channel.

When we get near the changing rooms on the beach, I change my mind about staying out of the sun. I think about putting on my bathing suit and sinking into the loud, endless gulf, cooling off in the water that looks like iced tea mixed with Windex. In my mind, there's a blue pineapple snow cone in my hand, too. I can almost taste its icy sweet tang. I almost ask Aunt Verona if we can stop. Sometimes we stop for a quick swim and a frozen treat at the Ocean Breeze Dairy Freeze. She keeps a beach tote in her trunk, with our swimsuits and flip flops and stuff. But if I ask, she might think I forgive her.

The beach is like a whole different country where anything can happen. For example, Mama and I took a walk on the beach early one morning when I was in the second grade, and we saw a giant sea turtle that had washed up to shore, dead. It was nearly as big as a Volkswagon bug, which I have proof of because we rushed home to get the camera. Mama lifted me up on top of it and took my picture, eight-year-old me, pretending to ride a dinosaur-size sea turtle. People think I'm lying until I show them that picture.

We've found other things on the beach, too. Like a coconut, which is amazing because it would had to float all the way across the deep blue sea to get here, unless somebody bought it at the Winn-Dixie and put it there as a joke. We found a shark's tooth, and an ancient coin. We also saw a giant, giant rattlesnake slithering out from the dunes once. Mama said it looked like a fucking anaconda. We find things that remind you how big, old and wild the world really is.

With the endless ocean under the open sky, you are also reminded that we are not much, in the overall scheme of things. Mama says walking on the beach is good when something is too big on your mind. But bad when you already feel like you ain't worth bothering about.

Aunt Verona pops in an eight-track tape and sings along, "Crackling Rosie," into the filtered end of her cigarette, like she's about to kiss it. She makes faces of passion and taps on the steering wheel.

There's a nomadic tribe that lives on the beach, that's what Mama calls them. Really, they're only beach bums. But they kind of are a nomadic tribe anyway. When I was in the fifth grade, Mama was talking to one of the tribal nomads on the beach, a tall, tattooed man with white-blond hair. They were talking about scoring, which can mean different things. There's scoring in sports, and on school assignments. "Scoring" also means making marks on something or an amount of time, as in "four score and seven years ago," or getting sex or dope. Mama got mad because I asked what kind of scoring they planned on, and listed the options. The tall man thought it was funny. He laughed like "Heh-heh-heh," showing his broken teeth. But Mama shooed me away, so I started picking up those teeny-tiny seashells that have the pretty colors on the insides, blue, pink, yellow. There's hardly ever no big shells.

The tall man suddenly grabbed Mama and started dragging her off somewhere, caveman style. Mama and I both started yelling. Then another tribal nomad, who goes by Slinky, showed up out of nowhere and knocked Tall Man out with a big old stick. Slinky is a pretty good name for Slinky. He slinked right up on Tall Man from behind and then whammo!

There's a pair of pink birds flying low over the water. Aunt Verona says, "Oh, my heavens. Would ya look at that." I don't answer her. She's a-gonna get the silent treatment for what she did to me and that's the way the weenie wiggles. That is the way the hot dog stands.

We go downhill, which is the seawall ending. The beach here is less crowded. Me and Mama's place comes into view a ways before we get to it. Besides being built on stilts, it's on a low mound too, set apart, all by itself. It's so steamy out today that our shack looks like it's shimmering in the sunlight, like a magical mirage from Walt Disney. Finally, we turn off Beach Drive and onto our shack's long, crushed oyster shell driveway. The sign out front is covered with a trash bag today. It has a picture of a bosomy cartoon mermaid holding a crystal ball. It says:

Madame Venice's Fortune-Telling Parlor
Come On In, Y'all. We Are Open!
A Tarot Card Readin' Is Only Two Buckaroos!

Aunt Verona turns off the car. Then she just sits there, staring at the shack, which makes me jittery. I fish around for my floppy straw sun hat, in the laundry basket that I tote my stuff in.

I put the hat on for protection, in case Aunt Verona slaps my head again. She lights a new Salem, then wobbles her head around like she's practicing a speech in her mind. She's waving her cigarette like a wand, trying to conjure up a good lecture, I guess. My mama says Aunt Verona is the only person she knows who can strut sitting down. Aunt Verona turns around to face me. My throat goes dry.

She says, "Your mama needs quiet and calm for a whole entire month, at the bare minimum. Start acting up and you'll drive her straight back to the hospital. And then you'll deal with Jesus, and me. You hear me, Miss Sassy?"

I say, "Yes, ma'am." Suddenly, I want Aunt Verona's take-charge attitude here more than anything. The last time Mama came home from the hospital, she was as brittle as thin glass, like even a loud noise would shatter her into a million pieces. If you take all the booze out of Mama's system, all that's left of her is a highly breakable shell. Drying out don't work on her. I say, "Can you come in with me? Please, ma'am?"

"Girl, you know I don't go in there. And there ain't nobody else to help her since she don't want to stay at my house. Go on, now. And mind your p's and q's."

Aunt Verona won't set foot in the shack because of the other aunts, the dead ones. Aunt Verona says they're the devil's work, which don't even make sense. The ghost aunties only get after you when you done wrong. Like Mama says, what kind of fucking devil would try to make you act *right?* I get out, lugging my laundry basket full of clothes and books along with me.

Aunt Verona backs the car down the crunchy shell driveway, with Johnny Cash crooning "Folsom Prison Blues" from the 8-track player. She cranks it way up, which hurts my feelings. I guess it's big whoopie time, now that I've been unloaded. Mama says Aunt Verona sure likes some down and dirty music, for a Bible thumper. But Aunt Verona says songs is just good fun.

After Aunt Verona's car is out of sight, I yank my hair out of the pigtails Aunt Verona always fixes it into, high up on my head like you'd do with a baby. I try to fluff out the kinks, then pull out a book of matches and a long Salem from the pack hidden in my laundry basket. I light up and inhale, like I'm trying to prove to myself that I really am still fifteen, not five. After a whole month with Aunt Verona, I'm not so sure.

Dizzy after stalling long enough to smoke two cigarettes in a row, I finally tiptoe up the stairs and into the shack. I go through the curtain that separates the fortune-telling parlor from the kitchen, and look down the hall. Thank god Mama's bedroom door's shut. My mama is loud and tough. Seeing her that last time she got dried out scared me to death. I'd rather have Mama drunk and yelling than breakable.

I'm gonna see if Katie wants to go hang out at Brown's diner. The ghost aunties can handle Mama better than I can anyhow. On the way out, I hear the background humming start, then the words "scobberlotcher" and "hoochie-coocher" tossed my way by the ghost aunties, who disapprove of young ladies roaming around on their own. The ghost aunties disapprove of just about everything. They're mad because they can't make me do nothing, so they call me names.

VERONA

By the time I turn onto my street, Crepe Myrtle Drive, I feel almost all better. I swan, Ajaja makes me ill. It starts with the shack I grew up in, where Venice and Jaci still live. Venice thinks fortune-telling is harmless, the same as Mama thought, when she was alive. But the occult ain't nothing to play with. And when you're somewhere that's already overflowing with all that mess in the first place, you ain't even playing with fire, you are playing with dynamite. But Venice don't listen.

Venice's first problem is that she's lazy. She'd rather court the devil than work a decent job. That way, she can lay around and drink and she don't have to take orders from nobody. And Miss Sassy is lucky a smack is all she got today, but there ain't enough smacks in the world to correct poor home training.

There's a very high concentration of wandering spirits on the island too, due to massive hurricane deaths. Many sour souls roam there, never having received proper Christian burials. Oh, I can't wait for the day when I never have to cross the bridge to Ajaja again.

I park in my garage, then go into the cool house, to the luscious aroma of garlic and oregano. My big floor candle has been moved from the corner of the living room floor onto the dining table, its five wicks lit, though nightfall is still hours away.

"Mama Mia!" Marty calls from the kitchen, where he's pulling a pan of lasagna out of the oven.

"Don't even start with me," I say, cheering up. He likes to tease me about being named after a city in Italy when I ain't Italian. Mama just liked the sound of the name. And ten years later, when Venice was born, Mama thought "Venice" sounded cute with "Verona." No one ever took much notice of it, except Marty.

Settling in at the dinner table now, Marty says a prayer in Italian, which he learned just so he could keep aggravating me. "Dio e' grande. Dio e' bueno. Ringraziamolo for questo cibo. Amen."

I lean around the giant candle to glare at him, because he'd be disappointed if I didn't. Duly chastised, he says our usual prayer, in English. "So, how's she doing?" he adds.

"I don't know. Venice didn't come outside. Our junior miss is getting a real smart attitude, though."

"Just like her mama," Marty says, then kind of cringes, like he wishes he hadn't said nothing.

"Ain't that the truth. I swan, Mama should have let us take Jaci in the first place. This is how babies raising babies turns out, all the way around." I draw a circle in the air with my fork.

"Your hands look pretty," Marty says.

My hands look the same way they always look. The same red nail polish and the same rings, wedding set on the left hand Avon ring on the right hand. He is trying to change the subject. The wooden bird in the wall clock pops out and starts sounding its hourly cuckoos.

Marty says, "It's Archie Bunker time," and pops out of his chair to turn on the television. I don't like the TV on during dinner, or Marty trying to change this subject every time it comes up. At forty-one years old, I've spent half my life trying to become a mother, while my baby sister had Jaci at just sixteen, with no daddy in sight. Mama let her keep Jaci instead of handing her over to Marty and I, like she ought to have. But look who's had to step in ever since, every doggone time another foolish mess goes on over there.

Marty busies himself adjusting the rabbit ears on top of our new color TV. Gloria and Meathead come into sharp focus, though Marty can't get rid of the green tint on the screen. It reminds me of the sky before a tornado.

VENICE

I hobble down the outside stairs like a ninety-year-old, holding onto the shaky wooden handrail. I'm shaky too, after a week of nothing but lying in bed and cooling off in the bathtub. Now there's a splinter in the palm of my hand, goddammit.

I hobble back up the steps and remove the splinter. Then I re-gather my stuff and try again. It would be nice to have a little help. Where the hell is Jaci, anyhow? Verona probably stole her again.

After making it down the steps, I uncover the fortune-teller sign, then ease into the lounging chair under the elevated shack. It's a shady, cushiony escape from the midday heat, with the breeze coming off the water.

Having lived here all my life, I forget that I live in paradise, or at least that's what my out-of-town customers tell me. The summer tourists don't see how it is here in the winter, though. Everything turns brown and gray. The whole island dies and ain't reborn until spring.

Then, the words desolate, forsaken and barren come to mind. Good crossword puzzle words.

The pink oleanders and red hibiscus really are beautiful right now though, and I smell some wild honeysuckle, too. there's also the roar of the surf across the street. I feel better here than anywhere else. I have been told it's because there is more oxygen by the ocean. I shuffle my tarot cards.

Wouldn't you know it, a big, showy pair of pink birds fly overhead. That is not a good sign, when you are fixing to do a reading about your future husband. I happen to know that them Ajaja birds do not mate for life. They pick a new partner every season. I don't strongly believe in mumbo-jumbo but when a big omen arrives right in your face, that's different. I work my tarot deck, one card at a time, feeling silly, like I'm back in school and scrawling boys' names on my notebooks. Feeling silly but doing it anyhow. *Will Dick ask me to marry him?*

I flip over the top card, the two of swords: a blindfolded man considering two choices. The man has to pick one of the choices, but he can't see. *Or he just don't want to see.*

No, that's in the past. Dick's all mine now. I put that card at the bottom of the deck and try again. *Will Dick propose to me this week?* I draw the six of staffs, which stands for good times, after hard times. That's more like it.

A car comes up the driveway, sending up a cloud of white dust. I shoulda left the damn sign covered. But I need money. The archeology professor from the university on the mainland gets out of the car. With his bulging eyes and boingy walk, he reminds me of a big frog.

"Hey there. How you doing, Prof?" I say with pep I don't feel. I have to be sort of nice to him because I love hearing about my land's history. Or maybe it's "our" land. I ain't sure who all's land it is. I've just always lived here. I pull my dyed red hair up off my neck, remembering I sorely need to touch up the roots. I say, "Ain't it a scorcher today."

"It does tend to be hot in the summertime, in sub-tropical Texas."

No shit, Sherlock? I always wonder if he means to talk down to me in particular or if that's just how he talks. "What can I do ya for, Prof?" I almost call him "Jeremiah," like in that "Joy to the World" song about the bullfrog.

"You may offer me a cold beverage," he says, like he's doing me a favor.

Well, yippee yie-yay cow patty! Ain't it my lucky day. I don't stock no drinks in my fortune-telling parlor, as he should know by now. But I need every dime. I say, "All I got is sweet tea, a quarter for a glass."

"That will do."

"Okay, hon. Follow me." I lead the way up the steps and into the shop, flip on the wall fan, then proceed alone, through the theater-style curtain to my living quarters. "Be back in a jiff," I call. My fortune-teller outfit hangs on a hook just past the curtain, on the kitchen wall: a purple satin bathrobe and the matching sleep bonnet that I wear as a turban, and a tray full of chunky silver jewelry. But it's too hot for all that shit today. Besides, the professor is only here to ask for the zillionth time if his students can dig on my property.

I return with the iced tea. "Here ya go. See anything else you want to buy around here?" I lean forward over the counter, displaying some cleavage. "Everything's got its price, ya know."

"No, I…I want to dog. I mean, I want to dig." His face pinkens.

I can't resist doing him like this whenever he stops by. My weird way of taking him down a peg or something, mainly.

He sets a quarter on the counter. "This is for the tea."

"Well, I should hope so! How cheap do ya think I am, bucko?"

His face turns a deeper shade and I feel a molecule sorry for him. "Just funnin'. Hey, want a reading? It's only two buckaroos."

"I am not superstitious."

"Yeah, me neither. Hold on, I got somethin' to show you." Perked up a little from the fun of picking on him, I rummage around in the rusty Folger's coffee cans under the counter. I keep some small artifacts that I find on my land in these cans, to show my customers. They are my proof that I'm not just making shit up, that there are layers of spirits all around this place, which bring about my special abilities.

It's partly true. There are definitely spirits here, if you count the ghost aunties. They don't give me no special abilities, though. They mostly just bitch at me. I hand him a mostly empty coffee can. "Since the last time you was here, there's a couple more teeth and bone burial beads. And them two little metal thingies."

He fishes a jeweler's loupe out of his pocket and peers closely at one of the items. "It says 'Charleston Slave Market, 1835.' That's a slave tag. All the way from South Carolina."

"A slave's lucky charm!"

"Certainly not."

I snatch it from him and thread it onto the silver chain around my neck.

He says, "That's not appropriate ---"

"That's what *you* think. What's that other little doohickey there?" I straighten my new pendant. I'll have to drop it into some vinegar later to see if I can shine it up.

There's a quiet spell, like he's never been disobeyed before and don't know what to do about it.

I'm getting bored. I say, "Ribbet."

"Pardon me?"

"Ribbet. Ribbet. Nothin'."

Finally, he looks through his loupe again, at the other little thingie. He says, "The Spaniards had a coin called 'pieces of eight,' because it could be cut into eight pieces, to spend in smaller increments. This looks to be one of those pieces."

"Pizzas of fate? It does look like an itty-bitty pizza slice."

"Pieces. Of. Eight."

"I heard ya. Just funnin'. How old?"

"Seventeenth or eighteenth century. Venice, irreplaceable knowledge is lost when artifacts are separated from their context. Now if you'd just allow the university to conduct a proper dig ---"

"No-no. I already toldja." I wag my pointer finger at him. I always say no, because I don't like him that much.

The ends of his wide frog mouth turn down.

I'm worn out. I say, "What can I send you home with? How 'bout a nice crystal to hang in your window? It'll make little rainbows all over the room when the sunlight hits it. Who don't need some rainbows in their life, huh? It's only two buckaroos."

He pulls two dollar bills out of his wallet, stuffs the crystal into his pocket, and boings sadly out the door. I sit down and lay my head on the counter, a short rest before I go out and cover the sign again.

From Professor Frog's earlier visits, I have learned that there is an old unmarked negro cemetery on my property, and rubble from a seventeenth century Spanish mission. There are also scattered, early native graves. It is goddamn fascinating. It used to be that when I found an artifact, I'd dig around it. But I stopped that, after my shovel clunked into a skeleton. I felt terrible for accidentally cracking its ribs. It was curled up on its side, with its little fists by its face. I tucked an old blanket around it, then covered it back up.

The professor said this area's supernatural reputation started with my pond. That was funny, coming from a frog man. I always stay clear of the pond, myself. I don't like fishing. I don't like mosquitos, cotton mouths, snapping turtles or gators, neither.

He said places that are thought to be "mystical" (he made air quotes with his fingers) always start with a fresh water source, like my pond. Then, if spiritual places like churches and burial grounds happen to be put there too, over time the place would get the mystical reputation. He said the great cathedrals of Europe had centuries of smaller churches and graveyards on their grounds first.

And before any of it, there was the water, always the water. It's something to think about.

But what smarty-pants Professor Frog misses is that it's not just what a place "gets a reputation" for having, it's what a place actually *has*. He don't even know that spirits are real.

The Jenson shack, my shack, was originally the old German farmers' church, built by one of my ancestors over a century ago. It's been rebuilt a couple times, after big hurricanes, but the layout stayed the same, according to the ghost aunties. The fortune-telling parlor is the old church room, and a storage pantry was converted into the indoor bathroom.

Then some male ancestor married a gypsy or a witch (depending on which ghost auntie is tellin' the story). That gypsy/witch is now ghost auntie Marvella, who denies everything, though nobody believes her. She was supposedly the one who turned the church into a fortune-telling parlor. By that time, the 1920's, the island had a decent tourist trade and fortune-tellers were all the rage. I wonder what the German farmers could have possibly grown here on this scrubland in the first place, though. I'll have to ask Professor Frog.

The professor always asks about my family history but I don't tell him nothing. I can practically hear the names the aunties would call him for that high and mighty attitude of his.

They'd thunder down, invisible, from beyond the air curtain. *Buffle head*, they'd shout. *Flop-doodle*. Maybe even *dummkopf.* I only hear a German auntie now and then, and real faint. It's been a long time since German was spoken here, among the living.

I shuffle my tarot deck. I'll do one more question, then I'll go downstairs and cover up the sign. When will Dick ask me to marry him?

The door chimes jingle. I shoulda covered the sign, dammit. But then, there's still that money problem. Ella Schmidt enters. I say, "Hey, gorgeous! How you doing?"

Ella is the sheriff's younger sister and a lifelong tattletale. I notice an old half-smoked joint in my ashtray. I slip the ashtray under the counter.

She says, "Gorgeous. Yeah, right. I'm making it, though." She takes a seat on a stool on the other side of the counter. She says, "And how are *you* doing?"

Oh, here we go. Nosey Rosey has come a'calling. "Can't complain. What can I do ya for today, hon?"

"I heard you got in a big old fight with your boyfriend. And then your big sister made my big brother take you to the hospital instead of the slammer."

"Well, guess ya can't believe everything you hear, huh? How about a reading? It's only two buckaroos."

"Did you really pull the toilet seat off in the ladies' room at the Blue Moon Bar? I heard you beat your fella with it." Her eyes sparkle with excitement.

I start laying out cards in the ten-card spread. Hopefully, she'll take a hint and drop the subject. But Ella wants the dirt. She says, "Is it true?"

It's hard to get mad at Ella because she don't know no better. She asks questions the way a little kid would, with no idea that you're supposed to be sly about it. She'd blurt out things like, "Who's your girl's daddy?" or "How'd you get that black eye?"

Ella looks so hopeful that I start confessing, against my better judgement. I say, "Well, I'm not a hunnert percent *sure* because I don't remember that night too good. But that *is* what I was told."

"Wowee! Well, I hope you're doing better now. Lookie here, I brought you some of my mayhaw jelly."

"Aw thanks, Ella. That's sweet. Ready?" I hold up a card.

"I am. But *please* don't tell nobody a word of this. It's a highly confidential matter."

"'Course not," I say. Ella's highly confidential matters are usually just her prattling on about whatever droopy old boy she has her eye on at the time. I ain't sure the poor girl's ever had a steady fella, though. I say, "What's his name?"

"His what? Oh, no. This is of a business nature."

"Oh. It's about your babysitting?"

"If you mean my home daycare, that is being converted into a home jail." Ella can sure get sniffy, for someone who's so pokey into other people's soft spots.

"Right. Home daycare, that's what I meant. Wait a sec. What did you say?"

"I said I'm starting a home jail. You know what, forget the cards. I just want your opinions, from the habitual jailbird perspective."

"I ain't a -- My fee is three dollars and fifty cents, for business consultations."

"Alrighty. Well, here goes. First, the island population has grown so much that the local jail ain't big enough no more. The deputies have to drive inmates to the mainland jail when our jail is full, which also leaves us a deputy short here on the island. And now the mainland jail warden wants to start charging our police department, when we use their jail."

"Mercy. Oh, and you can go ahead and pay me now, doll face."

"Doll face. I wish!" Ella hands over four one-dollar bills, which I put in the cash box. But I'll definitely give her the fifty cents change if she asks for it.

I am getting woozy. "Say, do you mind if I just lay down on the rug here while we talk? I don't feel so good."

Ella says, "Sure, go ahead. So anyhow, my brother says it makes more sense to just find more jail space here on the island. Oh, and there's a lot of trouble with our jail being mixed sexes, too. Did I tell you that? Them boys get all wound up and fight and stuff whenever there's a lady inmate there, even though the females are, of course, kept in a separate cell. Anyhow, long story short, my brother wants a separate, smaller jail for the gals. Of course, there ain't near as many gals getting locked up as men."

"Uh-huh. And this jail for the gals will be... in your house? Did I hear that right?"

In reply, Ella pulls some folded up papers out of her purse. "I have been awarded the contract. That's because very few people have my skills, first from taking care of Mama, then taking care of small children. Both are very challenging populations."

No, honey. You got the contract because you're the sheriff's sister. But I reach for the papers, from my position on the floor. After I look them over, I say, "I see. And you're wanting to put these gals in...does this say go-go dancer cages? What the hella, Ella?"

Ella looks proud of herself. She says, "Double-size go-go dancer cages. They're wide enough to lay down in. I saw them at that secondhand bar and restaurant supply place and thought they'd be cute."

This is loony as hell, even for Ella. I'm glad I'm on the floor where she can't see my face because it is hard to keep a normal expression on it. I say, "Okey-dokey, hon. Let's read through it all then, line by line."

By the time Ella leaves, I'm knackered. Whoever heard of a goddamn home jail. I slap a "50 cents" price sticker on Ella's mayhaw jelly and set it on the counter. If I don't catch up on my light bill this week, they'll shut off the damn electric again.

After going outside and covering the sign, I put a cold, wet rag on my aching head and go back to bed. I dream it's raining cool, refreshing sweet tea with bourbon.

JACI

Me and Katie Thomason stand on the side of Beach Drive with our thumbs out. We got to be friends in the last school year, in eighth grade Home Economics class. We sat next to each other, since the teacher seated the class alphabetically by our first names, and we're Jacinta and Katherine. Learning that the other one had flunked a year too gave us a special bond. I got held back because I got sick in the first grade and missed too many days. Katie and I agreed that our age difference made us more mature than the other girls.

The teacher was a crabby woman from England, who called us girls "bloody magpies" when we got on her nerves. Like that poor girl who sewed her hem inside out when we made skirts. Or the girl who squirted dish soap into her group's pot of boiling spaghetti noodles because she thought they ought to be clean.

Me and Katie figured Miss Stampen (Miss Tampon) was so mean because life had passed her by. Just imagine devoting your whole life to the domestic arts, then not being able to catch a man to perform any domestic arts for.

A station wagon pulls over. Katie says, "Let's go, magpie." I hang back, fighting the urge to run home. But after seeing that the driver is only an older lady by herself, I climb in the back seat, next to Katie. "Where to, girls?" the woman says, in a voice like she's pinching her nose while she talks.

Katie says, "The dime store in town, please. If you're going that far, ma'am."

The woman pulls back out onto the road. She says, in her fried voice, "You know girls, it's a good thing I stopped to pick you up."

"Yes, ma'am," Katie says. "Thank you."

"Oh, you don't have to call me 'ma'am.' I just go by Nancy. You know, a sex pervert could have stopped to pick you two up instead."

We ride along in silence for a while. Then the woman says, "Look, girls!" and pulls over on the beach side of the road. She points out over the water like she's never seen dolphins before. That means she ain't from around here, which I'm grateful for. The last thing I need is for Aunt Verona to hear that I hitchhiked.

When we're back on the road again, the woman says, "They're all over tourist towns like this, you know. The sex perverts. They just love young girls like you two."

"Yes, ma'am. I mean, Nancy," Katie says. Her wide-eyed gaze meets mine.

"They don't stop with just the connubial violation. No sirree, Bob. Why would they, when that would leave a witness? You know. The sex perverts."

A squeak escapes from Katie's mouth, which about kills me. I fake a coughing fit to hide my laughter.

Luckily, we're at the dime store now. The woman, Nancy, says, "They chop off the heads, you know, girls. And the arms. And the legs! With an ax. You know. So, the authorities can't identify the bodies."

"Yes, ma'am. Thank you for the ride," Katie says, scurrying out of the car.

The woman says, louder, "Then they throw the nekkid torsos out the car window, by the side of the road!"

I rush out after Katie, barely shutting the car door before we fall down on the sidewalk in a helpless pile of laughter.

Finally, Katie says, "Ready, sex pervert?"

We're there to buy embroidery stuff. Graffiti-like embroidery on your jeans is the in thing. In the store, there's three sizes of embroidery hoops. I say, "Let's get the medium." I pull two of them off the wall rack. I pick up a big pack of embroidery thread in all different colors, and a pack of assorted embroidery needles, too. "And we can split both of these, if you want."

"Give me that." Katie snatches the pack of needles and shoves it down the front of her shorts.

I feel my heart flip over in my chest.

"Stick the thread down your pants. Now! No one's around." Katie's face looks crazed, like she's a dangerous criminal. I just stand there, all froze up.

"Here," Katie says. She shoves the embroidery thread down the front of my shorts. She says, "Come on, now. I'll do the talking." I follow her to the checkout counter like she's got me on a leash. I don't have time to think it through.

A plump grandma type woman checks us out. "That'll be $2.50, honey," she says, and waits while we each count out our $1.25.

Back outside, I'm still in a state of shock. Katie says, "Got your thumb ready, magpie?"

"I'm just gonna walk."

"Why? What's wrong?"

"I just feel like walking, okay?"

"Oh. Well okay, sex pervert."

We walk single file down the road, me following Katie's bobbing ponytail. It's a long walk. I just hitchhiked and stole, both for the first time, within half an hour of each other. At this rate, I'll be shooting up heroin and robbing banks by next week. I decide to finish out the day I have planned with Katie, then start backing off from her. I thought she was more like me, not a red, red redneck but not a nothing-left-to-lose type chick, either. For a horrifying second, I think I see a naked female torso by the side of the road. But it's just a flattened cardboard box.

Back at the shack, we settle in at the picnic table on the covered deck. I draw a peace sign on my Levi cut offs and look over the embroidery thread colors. Katie draws a flower on her shorts.

I play it cool by not talking about what just went on, like I hitchhike and steal all the time and it ain't no thing to me. I ain't giving this chick a chance to go tell everybody I'm red or that she taught me anything I didn't already know. I say, "Are you sure you don't want to wear a pair of my shorts?"

"No thanks," Katie says, sitting there in her underwear.

A gauzy wisp floats in the air. It could be mistaken for smoke rising from our cigarettes but I know it's a stray ghost auntie, making her disapproval known. It's rare to see them, we usually only hear them. I think they just like to show off for company. I say, "I'll get some ice tea." I duck into the shack to check out what the rest of the aunties are up to.

The ghost aunties hum in the kitchen, with individual voices calling out, above the background drone. They don't approve of young ladies smoking. Good thing they didn't see what we did earlier. One of them tells me I'm just like my mama. Then I recognize my dead grandmother's voice, Meemaw Jo, calling me a disgrace, a chippie.

"Hush up, boo hags," I say, to cover my hurt feelings.

They hum louder. I worry that the ghost aunties' noise might break through the air curtain and reach Katie's ears. One thing about Katie, she's a blabbermouth. It's fun to hear what she says about other people but you don't want her to know too much of your business.

The air curtain, the invisible veil between this world and the next, ain't totally solid. Me and Mama can hear the ghost aunties, for example. And once in a while, other people can hear them, too. Of course, other people don't know that what they're hearing are spirits, but it makes me nervous anyway.

Sometimes I'm proud to live at the fortune-teller shack, other times embarrassed, depending on who's around. But it would be a whole different thing if people knew I live with real live ghosts. Everyone would think I was super weird. I'd be ruined. I go back outside with two glasses of sweet tea on ice.

Katie's blowing smoke rings up at the blue deck ceiling. She doesn't notice the wispy ghost auntie who's diving through the smoke rings, no doubt thinking herself hilarious.

I hand Katie her drink. She says, "Thanks, magpie. Hey, did you know people used to think a blue porch ceiling like yours kept ghosts out of the house? On the plantation field trip, they said the blue paint looks like water, and ghosts won't cross water, so it keeps them out."

Aunt Verona agreed that ghosts can't cross water. That's one reason she and Uncle Marty live on the mainland, even though Aunt Verona works here on the island. Uncle Marty works all over the place, because he has his own drywall business.

Mama says it's fucking stupid because the ghost aunties never go no farther than the deck anyhow. They never even go out into the yard.

The ghost auntie continues to float and flip under the blue porch ceiling, not slowed down by its color one bit. I swat her away. "Dang mosquitoes," I say. "Yeah. I went on a plantation field trip last year, too."

Katie turns back to her needlework. I am very relieved.

She says, "Did you hear about my sister, Linda?"

"I know who she is. What do you mean?" I'd heard about Linda having a baby out of wedlock. Everybody had, but it didn't seem polite to say so. I was super interested in stuff like that though, since I was born out of wedlock myself.

"It's a long story."

"Hold that thought, magpie." I go inside again and come back with a bottle of bourbon and two new names from the aunties: high jumper and wagtail.

"Are you sure bourbon goes with tea?"

"My mama drinks it all the time." I turn on the boombox to make sure Katie don't hear no ghost aunties. Freddy Fender croons about being there before the next teardrop falls. "Mama likes country music," I say, not wanting to seem red. "I usually listen to hard rock."

"Ha, leave it on, it's cool. Anyhow, Linda got pregnant when she was fifteen, same age as us."

I pull my embroidery work in close to my stomach. "Bummer."

"Yeah. Her weasel boyfriend said it wasn't his and he dumped her. So my mama sent Linda to a home for unwed mothers in Houston. Linda was supposed to give the baby up for adoption. But after Amara was born, Linda flat out refused. Even when my mama, the nurse and the nuns all ganged up on her.

"Wow, she's tough."

"Yeah. But then Mama said Linda couldn't come home, because Mama didn't want no little bastard in her house."

"She said that?" I sort of like thinking of myself as a bastard. It makes me feel exotic and mysterious, like an outlaw or a voodoo girl.

"Yeah. So Linda and the baby moved in with some creepy old dude. He was, like, thirty."

"Eww."

"Really. But now she lives in a trailer, just her and baby Amara. We can walk over there sometime. Linda's eighteen now. She can buy booze."

"Far out. Pretty name too, Amara."

"Yeah. Anyhow, when you meet my mama, don't say nothing, okay? I'm not allowed at Linda's. Mama says she don't want me picking up Linda's slutty ways."

I spot my mama's car weaving down Beach Drive. "Well, there's my mama and she's drunk. Let's book."

We hurry down the steps and across the back lot. Near the pond, Katie stumbles.

"Are you okay? Oh." We both notice at the same time that Katie's shorts are still in the embroidery hoop, back at the picnic table.

"What should I do?"

"It's too late now. Come on, magpie," I say, stepping up my pace again.

We pass an old black woman in a dress that looks like it's made from a burlap feed bag. The old woman points her tree branch walking stick at Katie's underwear, a silent reprimand.

After we get a safe distance from the old woman and recover from laughing, Katie says, "Wow. She just popped up out of nowhere. She looks like something from before the Civil War, like a ghost."

I wish Katie would quit bringing up ghosts. I say, "Oh, there's a few Black folks' shanties way down that dirt road over there. They go around selling fruit and vegetables and stuff. Mama lets them fish in the pond. Hey, you're wearing your Wednesday unders. It's Friday, you know."

Katie looks down at the lettering on her underwear. "Well, I didn't know I'd be running all over town in them. Linda's place is right down this street."

When Linda answers the door to her mobile home, she looks Katie up and down. "And here Mama thinks *I'm* the one who's hot to trot."

Katie turns around and moons Linda, who only sighs.

Katie says, "This is Jaci. She's a magpie."

"Magpie, huh. I don't know any Magpies. Is she BOI?"

"Yeah. Her mama was born here, too. Right, Jaci?"

I nod.

Linda says to me, "If I let you come in, do you promise to keep your pants on?"

I nod again, not sure if she's kidding or not. I'm tongue-tied because Linda is so beautiful. She looks like a life-sized Barbie doll, with her sweetheart face, long bleached hair and knockout figure.

Inside, a small girl watches us from the big cardboard box she's playing in.

"Hi!" I say. The girl ducks back into the box.

Linda holds up a purple bong, a question.

"Oh yeah," Katie answers.

We pass the bong and watch *Leave it to Beaver* on a portable black and white TV. I wave to Amara each time she pops out of the big box. The nearby kitchen counter is covered with dirty dishes and the kitchen trashcan overflows. I try to think of a polite way to leave, since the place stinks and I don't really like smoking weed anyhow. But after a few tokes, I kind of forget about it. I watch the orderly correctness of the Cleaver's TV household instead. It probably smells like Lemon Pledge or White Shoulders perfume.

Linda swoops up the little girl and takes her down the hall. I'm buzzed. I say to Katie, "You're melting," We both fall over on the couch, laughing because it was such a weird thing to say.

Katie says, "O-kay."

I get ahold of myself enough to shut up and not hurt Katie's feelings. But what I meant was that after seeing the gorgeous Linda, Katie seems like a melted version of her, with the face, nose and body all a little droopy here, a little squashed there.

Linda returns, wearing a tight black t-shirt that says "Blue Moon Bar" in swirly letters across a pale blue half-moon. She says, "I gotta go to work. Y'all can stay if you want. If not, Amara's okay. She'll just go to sleep." Linda goes out and shuts the door behind her. It kills my buzz. I say, "She leaves Amara home alone? Wait, that's not right. Is it?"

"Heck no, it ain't right. And she pulls this crap all the time. Amara can climb right of that crib now, too. I thought about telling Mama on her. But then Mama would know I was over here. I don't know about your mama but mine's meaner than shit when she wants to be."

"Man. That's a drag. Well, I guess we should stay here then, right?" I was scared of Aunt Verona, not Mama. When Mama and I fought, it was more like fighting with a sister and she was usually clumsy drunk then anyhow. Aunt Verona though, she could just look at you a certain way and make you feel like you barely even deserved to live.

Katie shrugs. "Yeah, I guess we kinda have to stay."

"Hey, it reeks in here. Want to clean?"

"May as well," Katie says, still shaking her head about Linda's poor parenting skills.

We turn on the radio and get to work. It's kind of fun to clean somebody else's place, like playing house. It's a lot more fun than cleaning your own dang place, that's for sure.

I stop for a minute when I'm vacuuming the hallway, to look in on Amara. She's adorable, asleep in her crib. I pretend that this is my life instead of Linda's. My trailer and my daughter, and nobody around to make me do a dang thing. A wild surge of joy catches me off guard.

A while later, we're done. We lay on the big ratty sofa, with our heads at opposite ends of it. I say, "Do you gotta call home?"

"Nah. It's Mama's weekend for overnight shifts. With Child Welfare. Linda don't have a phone anyhow. How about you?"

"Nope. We don't have a phone either, right now. Hey, my Aunt Verona works at the Child Welfare too. She hates the overnight shifts."

"Oh, is your aunt Verona Harris?"

"Wow. How did you know?"

"Verona" is not a name you hear every day, magpie. I might have heard something about her. But it's nothing."

"What? Tell me."

"It's no big deal. I just heard my mama say that your aunt is um, kind of bossy. Like they're at the same job level but your aunt acts like she runs the place."

I whack her with a pillow. "Oh my god. Like, tell me something I wouldn't already know."

We wake just before three a.m., to Linda counting her tips out loud at the kitchen table. "This place looks great," she says, like we ain't trying to sleep. "Thanks! Here's y'all's tip." Linda sets two dollar bills on the coffee table. "Oh, there's a mattress on the floor in the extra bedroom."

I grab my measly dollar and go off to sleep in the spare bedroom, glad to shut a door between myself and Linda. She might be beautiful but she's still trash, in my book. If I was lucky enough to have my own daughter and my own trailer, I'd damn well take care of them.

I've just finished making a peanut butter and banana sandwich when the door chimes jingle. Mama must have forgot to cover the sign before she went out. I peek through the gap between the curtain and the wall. Some long-haired dude is out there. "Be right there," I call.

I slip on Mama's fortune-teller outfit and jewelry, then push through the curtain and into the fortune-telling parlor, giving myself a pep talk. I want to make some money. Just do like Mama does. Just do like MeeMaw Jo used to do.

Acting like Mama, I say, "Need any help, hon?" *Hon? Oh my god.* An auntie titters, through the curtain made of air.

"You do tarot cards?" he says, like I didn't just say something idiotic.

"Sure. It's two buckaroos." *Buckaroos. How goofy.* He has a Yankee accent. I take his money and ask what his name is.

"I go by Chuck. I've seen you around and thought I'd drop in and say hey. Are you Madame Venice?"

"I'm her... assistant, Jaci." He came here to see me! And he was a fox, too. To start the reading, I deliberately pick the Strength card out of the deck. Mama says you should always start off with a compliment. The card shows a man petting a lion. I say, "This card represents you. It stands for strength and courage. Against an inner or outer struggle."

He touches the card. His fingertips touch mine.

I set up the ten-card spread, looking down at it, to hide my hot face.

As we work our way through the cards, I learn that he's seventeen years old and quit his junior year of school in Ohio a few months ago. He just rode off into the sunset on his motorcycle one day. It's one of the coolest things I've ever heard.

Mama says the last card should wrap the reading up with a "small bow," meaning send them off with some hope, but don't be goofy and overdo it.

Chuck's last card shows a picture of a devil, and it has the words "The Devil," written on it in big letters, just in case anyone had managed to miss it. *Dang it.*

Good thing I've seen Mama read the cards so many times. I look out the window, like something surprising is out there. When his gaze follows mine, I spin the card around real quick.

I say, "Ooh, the Devil card. But see, it's upside down. That makes its meaning the opposite of what the card says. Something good's on the way, for sure."

The door chimes clank and jangle. Mama stumbles in, drunk. She's grumbling about her boyfriend. It sounds worse than it is, since his name is Dick.

Just my dang luck. But maybe... just maybe, I can get Mama to keep walking, through the curtain and away from

Chuck. "Hi, Mama. I made you a sandwich. It's in the kitchen."

"Wha' the fuck you wearing? Whosis?"

Mercifully, Chuck mouths, "I'll see you later." He slips out the door.

I snatch up the cards and stomp to my bedroom, furious. Mama has a way of ruining things for me. I hear her crashing around in the kitchen now, carrying on some kind of argument with herself. The ghost aunties hum.

To drown out all of them, I play Lynyrd Skynyrd's "Free Bird" over and over on my boombox. Chuck from Ohio is as free as a bird. What I wouldn't give to be like him. No, to be with him.

I shuffle the cards and try to settle on a question. When he said he'd see me later, did he mean it for real, or was he just saying what people say when they leave somewhere? Is he thinking about me too? Will he be back?

I draw the Fool card. I re-shuffle and try again.

VERONA

I have three orders to deliver in Ajaja this evening. I can't seem to break away from this doggone place for the life of me. But, besides keeping my mad money jar full, being an Avon representative here helps me keep an eye on that sister of mine.

I know more than Venice thinks I do. I fix things behind the scenes when I can, too.

For example, there was that greasy bum she had living in the shack a couple of years back. He went by a name like Shoelace or Toenail or something ignorant like that. I found out about it because the bum's Mama's sister's friend was one of my best customers.

In the end, Marty bribed the bum away from my girls with $500 cash and a one-way bus ticket to somewhere in Wyoming or Montana, one of them big empty states, where the bum knew somebody.

Venice called me soon afterwards, crying about her boyfriend's mysterious disappearance, neglecting to mention that she'd lived with him in sin with my niece right there, or that he was well known around town for his criminal activities. I poured the sympathy on thick because the more I said, the harder Marty laughed. Marty says it's funny when I pull something because I'm usually such a goody-two-shoes. I'm not sure if that's a compliment or an insult. But as far as that phone call with my sister, it served her right.

I'm going to my least favorite house first. That woman buys a whole lot of products. I always try to get out of there before her husband gets home from work, in case he blames me for her spendy ways. She is friendly and easygoing, at least. Too easygoing, really. She's got a passel of unruly children and her house is always a disaster. Having to sit there smiling in the middle of that wild jungle as if it's normal, it frazzles my nerves.

Plus, one of her brats swiped a jar of my Hawaiian White Ginger cream sachet. That's an item that's very popular with the young girls. I had set it down on the sticky, cluttered kitchen table along with my other demonstration products, but it was no longer there after her two teenage daughters walked away. It still irks me.

The next time I went there, I gave each of them girls a sample packet of the Hawaiian White Ginger. I stared down each of them and squeezed their hands real hard, when I handed them the samples, telling them I knew it was something they liked. They stayed out of the kitchen during my visits after that.

So, I laid down the clean towel I've started bringing to her place. I arrange a pretty display of the latest items, on top of the towel. There's the Bicentennial soap dish set, the catch-a-star birthstone bangle bracelet, and samples of lipsticks, eyeshadows and perfumes.

"Oh. Oh, my," the woman says, eyes gleaming like a small child on Christmas morning.

Later, I'm figuring up the sales tax on her giant order, and she practically whispers, "Are y'all still wanting to adopt a baby?"

I nod but keep on with my calculations, feeling that strange robot attitude come over me.

Whenever the chance to get a baby comes up anymore, I find myself sort of shutting down at first. I feel like it's a small protection against further heartbreak, a gift from the Lord.

She says, "I have a delicate situation here. Can I trust you to keep it quiet, honor bright?"

I nod and she steps across the kitchen to shut the swinging saloon doors she's got between her kitchen and dining room. Then she keeps on looking at me.

"Oh, excuse me. Honor bright," I say, holding up three fingers as if I am taking the girl scout pledge.

She sighs heavily, then sits back down at the table. "Long story short, my daughter is expecting, and it's not a happy occasion."

"Oh, my goodness. I'm so sorry to hear that, dear."

"Thank you. I've sent her to my sister's in the hill country. The cover story is she's going there to be a mother's helper for my sister for a while, since she wasn't doing good in school anyhow. My sister has five small children. My husband don't even know the truth. Anyway, me and my daughter would much rather give the baby up to someone we know, than hand it over to Child Welfare. Oh, I'm sorry. I mean, I know you work for them, but you know--"

"I understand," I say, afraid to breathe, knowing how little it takes for these chances to disappear.

"Okay, so here's the thing. The baby's father is…"

Married, I think.

Black," she says.

My mind spins.

Of course, I was raised here in the south, in a time of segregation of the races that ain't completely over, for all practical purposes. But at the same time, I know that prejudice is unchristian. For us true Christians, anyway. And I want a child more than anything in this world.

She's probably getting tired of watching me sit here without speaking, like a ninny.

I say, "I'll have to talk to my husband."

"Sure. And believe me, if not, I understand. Just let me know. And remember, this is just between us, huh?"

I nod, then go out to my car. I turn on the windshield wipers instead of starting the ignition. She comes running out with my Avon suitcase, which I had forgotten all about.

All I can think of on the way to my next delivery is if the pregnant daughter is the one who stole my cream perfume. I rush through my other deliveries, eager to get home to Marty and figure this out. But by the time I finally turn onto Crepe Myrtle Drive, my own position on the matter is set: I want that baby.

Marty is quiet for a long time after I talk to him, like he's letting it all sink in, the same as I did.

Then he says, "Listen, it's 1976, not 1956, and I'm too old to care what other people think anyway. So it's up to you, babe. And, you know, there really wasn't any trouble in that way, with Jaci."

I crumple up the wrappings left from the burgers I'd picked up on the way home, toss them in the trash and started wiping down the table. "Jaci's father is Portuguese," I say.

Marty just shakes his head, and I realize that I've been saying that for so long that it no longer passes through my brain before it comes out of my mouth.

I don't even know who Jaci's father is. Venice refused to say. I would never have refused to answer my Mama if she asked me a question like that. But, in some small way, I've also always had a grudging respect for Venice for it.

Mama and I had had our theories and discussions about it but you can never be too sure in a tourist town. Mama was the one who started that bit about Jaci being half Portuguese.

The chance in front of Marty and me, to maybe, finally have a child of our own, seemed more real as the night wore on. I talked myself into a frazzled state. What if I wasn't the only one she'd asked? What if she promised the baby to someone else while I was sitting here twiddling my thumbs? I called at 9:45 p.m., telling myself it was okay to call since it was before ten, though the etiquette rule is really to call before nine.

When I was sure it was her on the other end, all I said was "Yes." I didn't say more than that, in case someone was listening in on an extension.

She said, "Perfect. And I'll see you in a couple of weeks, when you bring my Avon order, hon."

Marty and I decide not to tell nobody nothing. We've been through our adoption disappointments before and it's easier if other people don't know.

VENICE

I'm in a good goddamn mood, getting ready to go to the Fourth of July beach bash with my honey. Whatever else people might say about Dick and I, the sparks fly between us. There's no denying that. Our relationship is like the sparkly fireworks we'll see tonight, set off from a barge way out in the Gulf.

One time, Dick said we ought to try out for that TV show *Love, American Style*. The short skits crack me up, starting with fireworks, then fading to dark after each crazy love disaster. That's us, all right.

Hopefully, next year at this time, Dick and I will spend July fourth at our own home together, away from the crowds. Maybe with a few friends over and some fresh shrimp tossed on the grill.

This is the third time around for Dick and me and it's the best time around. I feel there's truth to the saying "three's a charm." Now that Dick finally left Boring Barbara for good, he seems calmer. I'm less hot-tempered with him too, since he no longer keeps me hidden away like our love is a dirty story out of the *Penthouse Forum*.

I want one of them taffy-colored homes in that ritzy new subdivision, Sunset Reef, with the outside of its houses painted in pastel colors like mint green or peach. My scrapbook features examples of the posh type of home I dream of, done up in aquamarine and cream inside. I'd entertain the members of the Sunset Reef Ladies' Club in my own built-in swimming pool, overlooking the bay. I might even have a

31

part-time maid to bring out fancy cocktails and hors
d'oeuvres, while my new friends and I work on our
Coppertone tans and watch the pleasure-boats glide by. Scenes
from the new life I'm planning play through my mind like
scenes in a movie, picking up more detail each time around.

I get dressed while I wait for the hot rollers in my hair
to cool. I step into my denim miniskirt, then carefully pull my
new red, white and blue sequin tube top over my curler-
covered head. Last are my platform flip flops, and the
turquoise pendant Dick bought me on our trip to Las Vegas. I
slip it onto my chain, next to the slave tag. I'll have to
remember to show that to Dick. What a hoot.

After getting a glass of sweet iced tea from the kitchen,
I head back to my bedroom to get the bourbon from its hiding
place in my closet. I feel a little tipsy already, just from
knowing it's on the way. Not drinking at all don't suit the life I
have planned, and that's that.

Dick don't want another Boring fucking Barbara. And
when they've put a man on the goddamn moon, it's just
fucking stupid to think people can't limit how many cocktails
they pour down their own throats.

Like Dick says, you just got to pay attention. One drink
per hour, no more. And no less. I take a big sip and wait for
the luscious calm to settle over me. But something is off. I
open the bottle again and sniff, then taste. This bottle is filled
with pure goddamn water. Pissed off now, I shout, "Jacinta
Josephine Jenson!"

JACI

I slam my novel shut and toss it across the bed. I'm
reading *One Flew Over the Cuckoo's Nest* and I don't
appreciate being interrupted right when McMurphy gets
lobotomized.

I can't stand hearing my full name anyhow. It reminds
me of that children's song "John Jacob Jingleheimer
Schmidt." Whenever we go out, the people always shout, there

goes John Jacob Jingleheimer Schmidt. Jacinta Josephine Jenson Shit. So square.

I go to Mama's room so she'll quit yelling and then I see the water-filled bourbon bottle on the dressing table. Whoops. I had forgotten all about that. But I get mad right after I get scared. After everything she's put me through with her own damn drinking, who the hell is she to yell at me?

Mama's got her makeup mirror set to the evening setting. She's curling her eyelashes, ignoring me now, after she just interrupted me. What kind of mother sits in her bedroom drinking in the daytime, or even getting ready for a *date.* And she's wearing a miniskirt. And a tube top? Oh my god.

It's nearly as sickening as thinking about Mama and Dick doing it, which I have to hear from my bedroom when I'm trying to sleep. They're too old for that. I hope Dick breaks his frail old wiener bone. I hope it snaps off and rolls under the bed.

An auntie calls out, "Mutton dressed as lamb!"

That's exactly what Mama is. I join in with, "Ewe!"

Mama halfway smiles. She doesn't get the joke. She probably thinks I'm sticking up for her, saying "Ew!" about the auntie's remark or maybe "You!" as if the auntie is the one who's desperately trying to look younger than she is.

Mama looks up from her mirror, like she wants to be friends, after she was just ready to take my head off two minutes ago. She must have found something else to drink. I don't know that she'd drink Listerine or cough syrup but I don't know that she wouldn't, either. I don't smile back. I say, "Baa!" still going with the sheep theme.

An auntie laughs, above the background hum. Meemaw Jo calls out: is *As the tree inclined, so the twig is bent.*

"Bug off, banshees," Mama yells.

So the twig is bent? "What the heck did I do?" I call to the aunties, hurt, since I had just taken their side.

Mama's back to being mad again now. She holds up the bourbon bottle. She says, "That was real cute. Now go outside and get me a switch."

I glare at her.

"I'm not telling your smart ass again. Get out there. Now."

The aunties' hum. One of them says, *Ah, you're both slatterns. Malt worms!* Another one whispers, *Schlampen,* whatever that's supposed to mean.

I leave the room, pass through the curtain and out the door, then stomp down the steps, rattling the whole crappy house. I come back with a branch, stripping its leaves and throwing them on the floor as I go. Mama tries to take the switch but I decide to hold on to it.

We fall onto her bed, fighting over it. She says, "You'd best goddamned give it to me right now. PDQ."

I say, "You're the one who deserves a goddamn whipping."

She's right, you know, Meemaw Jo calls out.

Mama says, "How would you like me to leave this goddamn dump for good, and you with it, huh?"

The words burn like fire. Mama's never said anything like that before. She stays gone too long sometimes, but then she acts like it was an accident or something. She tries to make it up to me, taking me to the show and shopping and stuff.

I yank hard and pull the stick out of Mama's grasp. "Dick's a dick and you both make me sick," I sing, snapping my fingers on my free hand. The aunties stop humming for a long minute, then they howl with laughter. The aunties will be on your side one minute and turn on you the next.

While I enjoy their rare approval, someone grabs the switch from behind me. I yank it forward in response, like, automatically, and the other end of it lands on Mama's forehead, hard.

Thwack!

I didn't mean that!

The someone who grabbed at the switch turns out to be Dick. I didn't hear him come in.

Who said he could just walk right into our house?

Mama sweeps herself out of the house, arm up over her forehead, like a damsel in distress in the old talkie films I watched on a TV special one night, with Aunt Verona and Uncle Marty.

Mama likes to act delicate in front of men, when she remembers to. If he wasn't here, she'd come after me with a shoe or a hairbrush, screeching threats and bad words.

Dick calls after Mama. "Are you all right, sweetheart? Sweetheart?"

Like it wasn't all his dang fault in the first place. I repeat something Mama said when she was mad at him. "Now Dastardly Dick thinks he's Dudley Do-Right."

Dick looks around, trying to figure out who's laughing. A fresh chop lands on his head.

I cradle the switch, smiling sweetly.

A lone auntie screams with laughter. I think it's Meemaw Jo. I hope so.

Dick grabs the switch and hits me back! He lands a sharp crack on my head.

The aunties' humming rises to a loud buzz, like a swarm of hornets, which makes me feel loved. Dick looks around the room, eyes wide, then rushes out.

I go out on the deck as the Dick gets into his convertible. Its canvas top is down. Mama waits in the passenger seat, a southern magnolia in need, hair pulled back to display the new goose egg on her forehead. I fling the switch over the deck railing. It bounces off the car's shiny red hood. Yee-haw!

Dick yanks his car door open like he's gonna come after me, but Mama says something to him and he shuts it again.

Now I'm furious about the drama below, at how I've somehow become the villain. It's not fair. I have the worst mother in the world. She's the villain, not me. I scream, "I hope you die, Mama. I hope you die!" There. Let's see how she likes that.

Mama don't even look up. She just delicately dabs at her face with Dick's handkerchief.

The car backs down the oyster shell driveway, then speeds down Beach Drive, headed to town.

Gem-colored fireworks bloom against the black sky over the Gulf. I sit on a log by the fire, on the stretch of beach that's left to us teenagers. Katie and Linda sit beside me, one on each side. The sisters ooh and aah at each new kaleidoscope burst. I nod along with them but my mind is stuck on earlier in the day, like a phonograph needle stuck in the groove of a record album. *I hope you die Mama, I hope you die Mama, I hope you die...*

My thoughts and the head injury from Dick combine with the heat to crowd out my oxygen. I breathe as deep as I can but I can't get enough air. Some fool always builds a fire on beach party nights, even in super-hot weather like this. But we didn't bring a blanket to sit on, so to move away from the fire, I'd have to sit on sand, in my white shorts.

"You okay?" Chuck shows up, out of nowhere.

It's so much worse, with him here. People have started gathering around to watch me gasp for air. Oh, great. Just what I always wanted, to be a spaz in front of the guy of my dreams.

"Here, babe. See if this helps." He hands me his beer.

I take a sip. Then another. I somehow manage slip off the log, hitting the back of my already sore head on it, on the way down Just when I thought it wasn't possible to be any more ridiculous.

"Do you want to go home?" Katie says, sharply, like a slap.

"Just let me die in peace, maggot," I snap back.

"What did you call me?"

"Magpie. I meant to say magpie. Sorry." Still a little mad and a little out of it, I go ahead and gave Katie a hard four-fingered jab, pretending I'm sticking a giant fork in her side, her punishment for being mean to me.

"Ouch!" What is wrong with you?"

I fell over on the ground, showing that I am too out of it to be held accountable for my actions. *There,* I think. *Ha!*

"Just leave her alone," Chuck says to Katie.

Katie glares, first at him, then at me.

"She can rest here for a while. I'll get my sleeping bag," Chuck says.

Katie says, "That's okay, Dr. Demento. We've got her." But he was already gone.

I kind of like being fought over but I say, "It's okay, magpie. I know him."

Chuck comes back and makes me comfy on top of the sleeping bag he's brought with him, farther away from the fire, behind the log Katie and Linda are sitting on. He even brings me a rolled-up towel for a pillow.

A tall, skinny guy walks up to Linda. He says, "Hey there. Got a light?"

"No," Linda says, kind of rudely.

Katie says, "I do." She lights his cigarette but his gaze stays on Linda.

"Uh, cool fire," he says, to Linda. He stands there for a while, ignored, then shuffles back the way he came.

Linda looks at Katie and holds her nose, like the guy stunk or something. I feel kind of sorry for him. I go back to watching the fireworks.

Another guy comes over, a beefy jock type. "Do I know you from somewhere? You look familiar," he says to Linda.

She bugs her eyes out.

Katie says, "Hey, I know you. Don't you live over on Oyster Bay Road?"

He nods to Katie, but speaks to Linda. He says, "Whoa! Look at that," about a multi-blooming firework in the sky. After getting no answer, he drifts away, too.

Linda holds her nose again. Katie shakes her head.

Before long, yet another guy approaches Linda. Her bright, bleached blonde Barbie hair draws attention, even at night. I'm glad Chuck don't seem to notice her. When he goes to get more beer, I sit up and say to Linda, "Aren't you gonna talk to any of them?"

"I doubt it. I don't like dudes who I don't know."

But then how could she get to know anybody, if she wouldn't even talk to them? Before I can ask, Linda and Katie go off to mingle in the crowd. Chuck and I talk, lying side by side on the sleeping bag. He tells me about his hometown in Ohio. We don't talk about Mama.

The crowd thins. The fire burns down. He lays next to me, a grown man on his own, not some school-boy. We kiss, drink, and talk some more. He lights two Marlboros and hands me one. I say, "You remind me of the Marlboro Man, but on a motorcycle instead of a horse."

Then I cringe, mortified.

He laughs, though. His voice is deep and his dimples make me swoon. I trace them with my finger, and he laughs again. I slip his Zippo lighter into my pocket, a souvenir from the best night of my life so far.

Later, I wake to Katie telling me to get up. Chuck sits up next to me. He must have fell asleep, too.

Katie scolds me all the way home, making me answer questions about if I want to get a reputation or end up like Linda.

Funny how Katie is criticizing how I act, when I had been ready to get rid of Katie because of how she acted. I say, "I guess we're both dirty birds then. Huh, magpie?"

"Both? What the hell did I do?" Katie says. "I'm not the one acting like a big fat Linda."

I elbow Katie to shut her up, since Linda is right there. But Linda chimes in, cheerfully agreeing with Katie.

When we reach the shack, I say good-bye and tiptoe up the steps, into the fortune-telling parlor, then through the curtain.

The house is quiet. The aunties are weirdly silent, even though I've come home so late.

I go into Mama's bedroom. The dresser drawers are nearly empty. The closet has been cleared out, too.

Mama is gone.

September, 1976

JACI

I wake to pounding at the door. Chuck scrambles out of bed and steps into his jeans.

From out on the deck: *Knock, knock.* "Venice Pearl!" *Knock, knock.* "Jacinta Josephine!"

I scramble to get dressed.

From out on the deck: "Open. This. Door!"

The aunties start up against me, even though all I was doing was sleeping. *Shame. Jezebel. Saddle goose!*

I pull the attic stairs down from the ceiling, wincing when they creak. I tiptoe up, motioning for Chuck to follow me. He does, then carefully pulls the steps up behind him. He says, "Is that your Aunt Verona?" as we settle in on the dusty attic floor.

"Yeah. And she *never* comes any farther than the driveway."

"Oh hell. You gotta be careful, babe."

"Well, like I told you, Chuck, Linda said I'd be a legal adult if I just got married."

"Shh. Keep your voice down." He crawls over to the attic window and looks out. "I think she's alone, at least."

"That's okay. You don't have to marry me if you don't want to."

"Hey, now. I didn't say that. Damn, doesn't anybody ever clean up here?" he says, dusting off his pants.

"I know plenty of dudes who would, you know."

"Plenty of dudes who would come up here and clean? Great, let's call 'em."

"I'll call 'em, all right."

"Come on. We've already talked about this. It's too soon for that."

"Okay, Upchuck."

"That's not very nice."

"You're not very nice."

"Yeah, I see how grown up and ready-for-marriage you are. Hey, did you hear someone laugh just now?"

"No!"

"Okay, damn. Keep your voice down."

From outside, loudly: "I swan. If I get one more call from the school, I *will* be calling the authorities."

Aunt Verona stomps down the outside steps hard enough to shake the place. Her car peelsout. "It Wasn't God Who Made Honky Tonk Angels" blares from the car's 8-track player.

An auntie says, Miss Sassy will be in the pudding club before you know it.

"Did you say something?" Chuck says.

"No, Charles Manson. Hearing voices is a sign of insanity, you know." I feel lousy right after I say it.

He draws in his breath. "You know something, sometimes you really do seem like afifteen-year-old."

I would have been mad, usually, but I feel better now that he hurt my feelings back, after I mocked him about hearing voices. Now we're even. I pinch where his boobs would be if he was a girl, trying to lighten the mood.

It works. "I swan!" he says, in a high-pitched voice.

I giggle. "My aunt thinks "I swear" is cursing. Once, when I was little, she yelled at me once for saying I had to use the bathroom."

"What were you supposed to say?"

"I think I was supposed to say, 'powder room.'"

"Your aunt sounds like a barrel of laughs."

"She is. We laugh at her all the time." I feel a twinge of guilt, then. At least Aunt Verona never leaves me, even though sometimes I wish she would. I say, "Oh, she's all right."

"Yes. Let's remember who the truant juvenile delinquent is, in this story. Since Aunt Verona is not here, I better spank you for her." He pulls me over on his lap, and I shriek with laughter, until the aunties start humming.

VERONA

My world is falling apart. Venice and Jaci are gone. Gone! Now, Venice running off ain't nothing new. Marty thinks now that Jaci is a little older, Venice is just treating her like a pal instead of a daughter, and they're off having a ball together. I can definitely picture that, because Venice is very immature. That would not be a relief though, as Marty seems to think, since Venice's idea of having a ball includes all manner of things immoral, illegal and dangerous. I can't stand to think about Venice off on some crazy drinking binge, with God knows who, and Jaci right there with her.

Marty and I try to find them. It's become the focus of our life. We drive by the shack, talk to whoever we can think of who might know something, and regularly call the jail and the hospital. I go to church every day I can, to pray for their safe return. I swan, church is the only thing keeping me sane.

Marty thinks we ought to call the law. But then, they ain't his blood relatives. It would be different if we had cause to believe they'd been kidnapped or something. But, considering the most likely scenario here, all the law would do is make our family business public. Or catch them and lock them up, since there's no telling what Venice might have on her. And Jaci is not in school, which I believe could get her sent to juvenile hall right there. I don't see how being caged up with criminal trash would make either of them come out better.

No, it's better to handle our own, on our own. And I'm here to tell you, I do plan to handle it. I will be taking Jaci when I find her, and that's final.

Also, our adoption fell through. It was awful to go through again. The girl gave birth soon after we agreed to take the baby. I didn't know she was that far along. It was a healthy little boy, who looked just a touch ethnic, like Jaci. We'd have taken him anyway but if people would have believed he was Portuguese, we'd have let them believe it.

We drove four hours to the hospital, way out past Austin. After we stopped to look at that precious baby through the glass in the nursery, I wanted to speak to the birth mother, who was still there in the maternity ward. I wanted to tell her she'd be welcome to visit once per year, as long as there weren't no problems with it. I wanted to allow the birth mother and our son to know each other just enough to take away the pain of not knowing anything.

Anyway, this old, and I mean ancient, black gal barges into the maternity ward, wearing a bonnet and a long, homespun dress that looked like something straight out of the last century.

She used a tree limb as a walking stick to steady herself with one hand and dragged this big, thirty-ish, light-skinned black man along, with her other hand. I mean, she was pulling him along by his ear. It would have been funny if it wasn't so pitiful.

After announcing herself as Henny Johnson, the old woman starts yelling. "You people ain't taking another one of our'n! That baby's daddy is alive and present, and he do not consent to give that baby away! Ain't that correct, Royal?"

"Yes, ma'am," the big lunk muttered.

The next thing we knew, there was nurses and security guards and social workers buzzing around all over the place.

We had to wait in an office, on a different floor of the hospital. An hour later, we were told that the man and his grandmother had taken the baby home. Besides having my heart broken again, I still cringe when I think about how poor they looked. What kind of life can they offer?

I swan, some days I just don't even want to get out of bed. Oh, Marty and I both noticed that the baby's father had a spot on his head where his hair grew in white, the same as Jaci does.

Of course, that don't prove nothing for sure. And even if it did, I don't see how it would help Jaci to know nothing about it. It might be 1976 but it *is* still the south.

VENICE

I feel better after some aspirin, a big glass of water, and more sleep. Freshly showered, I wash my bathing suit in the bathroom sink of our motel room. I swish it around in the sink in soapy water. "This goddamn suit smells like mildew."

"You're not innocent, either. Look here." Dick traces a long scratch down the side of his face, with his index finger. "You see that? And what about this, huh?" He shows gouge marks where I guess I must have dug my fingernails into his wrist.

"Excuse me, but I asked you to pick up a few things at the store, and then I was talking about washing my bathing suit. And that is all I said to you. So, what is your fucking problem? I can't go to the store myself because people will gawk at a black eye and I ain't in the mood for it. Okay?"

"Oh. Okay then."

"And while you're out, can you get me a pair of sunglasses and a newspaper? When you get back, let's take a dip in the pool."

"Today's a new day, then?"

"Mmm-hmm." He'd said Boring Barbara could hold a grudge for years. I don't want to be like Boring Barbara.

After he leaves, I think about calling Verona. I ought to just buck up and get it over with. She might not even be mad. After all, she's got Jaci, like she always wanted. I've thought about calling every day for the past few weeks but it gets away from me. I'd rather come back with a diamond ring on my finger. Maybe even with a new house. I want to return as somebody better, after all this.

I can't return with a black eye anyway. Maybe I should wait another month anyhow, give Jaci time to get used to her new school. Jaci probably wouldn't even want to leave Verona's house then. Maybe things would just work out for the best, all around.

What I ought to do is just have a drink and calm down. Oh right, we're out of booze, dammit. Dick will be back with

it soon, though. It's on my list. I turn on *Medical Center*.
Right now, I'll have to settle for a dose of the handsome TV
doctor, Joe Gannon.

Two hours and a half a pack of cigarettes later, Dick
still ain't fucking back. *This shit again.* I feel real shaky. I
check all over the room again but there's no booze and no
money.

I pull on a pair of cut-offs and a t-shirt, over my now
dry bikini and head to the motel bar. I drop in there sometimes
when Dick's at work, or wherever else Dick fucking goes.

The place is empty, aside from the old biker with the
beard, on his usual stool at the far end of the bar. The
bartender named Bud is on duty, a fiftyish guy with a pot belly
and maybe a little crush on me. I sit at a table, because a gal
sitting at the bar alone looks cheap.

"What can I get you, gorgeous? Sweet tea with a shot
of bourbon?" I peek up at him, all shy-like, aware of my black
eye. "Could I just, could I trouble you for a glass of water?"

"No trouble at all. Ooh. Are you all right, sweetheart?"

"As good as can be expected. You know."

He brings me a glass of ice water and a tall drink, just
like I was hoping for. "A double iced tea and bourbon on the
house for you, my dear."

"Oh! Now you didn't have to do that. You're the dear.
Thanks a bunch." He remembered what I drink. It's nice to
have someone to turn to in a pinch. When he goes into the
back, I grab a basket of pretzels and peanuts off the bar. I'll
have to keep our room stocked better.

When I finally get back to the room, Dick is there. On
the dresser is: a jar of Jiff peanut butter, crunchy. A loaf of
Wonder bread, a carton of Winstons, two bottles of bourbon, a
box of tea bags and a box of sugar. Dick says, "Sorry, babe. I
had some business to take care of."

"You could of called at least, goddammit. Did you get
me any sunglasses? And what's this, green tea? You know I
like the regular Lipton." I fill the electric kettle with water and
plug it in. "Green tea tastes like grass clippings and piss."

"Sorry, babe. That's all they had. And I tried to call.
Many times. I couldn't get through to the room." He spreads
his arms, palms up. "Where were *you*?"

He does that palms-up thing when he's lying. It's
followed by that trying-to-turn-it-all-around thing. It's all just
fucking hopeless. I say, "Just go fill up the ice bucket before I
kick you in the ass. Dick the dick. You make me sick."

"Missing Jaci again, huh?" he says, grinning like we're
friends again. When he turns around, I go ahead and do it, kick
him in the ass. It hurts my bare foot and I hop around, cussing,
which makes us both laugh, because we ain't got much sense.

"Did you bring me some green stamps, at least?" He
hands them over and I start licking a sheet of them to stick into
the book, while he goes for the ice. I've got my eye on a fancy
cheese and cracker serving set in the green stamp catalog, for
entertaining, when Dick and I get a place of our own. It has a
little built-in drawer for the cheese knife.

At the washateria last week, I took a quiz in a
Cosmopolitan magazine someone had left there, "Are You in a
Love-Hate Relationship?" The results, 18/20, assured me that
I am. I take a swig of bourbon, then flop down on the bed,
waiting for the teapot to whistle. I'll straighten him out later.
I'll fucking straighten everything out later.

JACI

As we get closer to Halloween, the veil between the
living and the dead thins. The aunties' voices break through
air curtain more now.

"Can you fill out some applications today, babe?" I say
as Chuck comes into the bedroom, just out of the shower.
Chuck going out for a while will give the aunties a chance to
calm down. He needs a break from them, too. He keeps telling
me he hears voices. I always tell him I do too, but that it's just
the birds outside or the surf across the street or whatever else I
can think of.

I start to light a cigarette but the aunties hum, so I slide
it back into the pack. Any little dang thing at all makes the
aunties hum now, even Chuck lighting a cigarette.

"Didn't you have any customers this week?" Chuck asks. He's rooting through the top dresser drawer for matching socks.

"Just one. Like I said before, the regulars will only tell their business to Mama. The summer tourists are gone and the snowbirds ain't here yet."

"What happened to the money you had, though?"

"Golly gee, let's see… hot dogs, bread, mustard, oranges, soap, cigarettes, rubbers, light bill?"

"Thanks for the sarcasm. Anyway, I am gonna check back with a couple of places I already applied at. On the way home, I'll stop by the bay and gather up a bucket of oysters, and try to sell them to the Shrimp Shack. So that'll be a couple of bucks. Wait, did you say "rubbers?" The rain boots kind or the good kind?"

"Wouldn't you like to know?

"Hell yes, I would like to know. So… did you change your mind?"

"Not yet. Just wanted to see if you were listening."

He gives me a hard look. It makes me swoon. He's super foxy when he's mad. He splits, and I start chopping up a salad for supper. The aunties approve of fixing dinner. After this, I'll read. They also approve of reading. Aunt Verona gave me a secondhand set of encyclopedias at the end of the last school year and my goal is to read them all.

I just started on volume three, of the set of thirty-three. I read for an hour or two during the day and again at night when I can't sleep, when the rest of the world goes quiet and thoughts of Mama get loud in my mind. I'd give anything if I could take back my last words to her: *I hope you die, Mama.* When I finally do drop off to sleep, sometimes my dreams turn to nightmares. Sometimes it's like the fairy tales Meemaw Jo used to read me, were I'm left in the woods like Hansel and Gretel. Other times I just fall and fall, with nothing there to catch me.

But then I'll wake up and Chuck will be asleep next to me and I don't have to go to school, and then I can't believe my amazing great luck. Katie says everyone at school is super jealous.

The sound of a delivery truck outside cuts into my thoughts. Two men are out there, unloading big boxes from it. The yearly order's here, finally. Mama goes to a big wholesale bazaar up north once a year and places one huge order. She gets lots of discounts from buying in bulk, but the delivery is slow. I can practically hear Mama now, pitching a fit. "A lotta good all this oogie-boogie bullshit will do me, now that the goddamn summer's over," she'd say.

"Goddamn four-flushers. Tin Jesuses, second generation vipers!" Mama called people the craziest names. Half the time, I didn't even know what they meant, just like with the aunties' name-calling.

I unpack boxes. Staying busy calms my mind. I arrange boxful after boxful of merchandise on the parlor shelves: tarot decks, crystal balls, angel necklaces, love potions, Ouija boards, dreamcatchers, and a half shelf full of Linda Goodman's *Sun Signs*.

"What's all this?" Chuck says, scaring me. I didn't even notice the door chimes. He slaps some bills down on the counter. "Money as promised, sweet cheeks."

"This is the yearly delivery, at long last. And thank you for calling me a name that includes my face and my ass at the same time. You may as well just call me a cloaca." I'm trying to be funny but the faint hum starts up and ruins the moment. I grit my teeth and make a mental note not to say "ass" anymore.

"What the hell's a cloaca?"

"Nevermind. Let's take a walk after supper, okay? I want to get out of the house for a while." I want to talk to him, out of the aunties' earshot. We eat salad while I make grilled cheese sandwiches. Me at the stove, Chuck sitting at the table. Happiness runs through me in a wave. Acting like I'm Chuck's wife makes me crazy happy.

We walk over to the beach. It's balmy out, that's the word. The sun's set and the air is scented with sweet flowers, wild honeysuckle or jasmine. Way out in the Gulf, the row of ships waits to get into the ship channel. The whole scene makes me think of exotic, faraway places, like any kind of magic could happen.

I say, "We should get out of the shack for a while, before my aunt shows up again. And before the truant officer or Child Welfare show up." *And before the aunties' moaning and groaning sends you to the psych ward.* I've thought about just telling Chuck about the ghost aunties. But Mama and Meemaw Jo had always told me it just ain't something you tell people.

They wouldn't understand.

He says, "We've talked about this, right? I guess we could find somewhere to pitch my tent or go to that old fishing shack on the bay that you talked about. But either way would be a lot less cushy than the shack. And we'd probably have more of a chance of getting caught, too."

It hurts my feelings that he'd rather live like swamp rats than marry me but I already decided not to bring up marriage anymore for a while. I say, "I want to ask Linda if we can stay with her. I could watch her kid for her." A small sand dollar is lying in the sand. I pick it up. You hardly ever find a whole one.

He doesn't answer for a while. Nervous, I draw a heart in the sand with my finger. Finally, he says, "Linda's, huh? Well, it would be better than roughing it. But I think we should just keep doing what we're doing for now, babe. Just stay inside. with the doors locked and the curtains closed. Keep the radio and TV volume low, that sort of thing. We can get a different place after I find steady work."

I've made up my mind, though. "I want to go, now, babe." I draw J + C in the heart.

"All right, all right. If it'll make you happy."

"I'll talk to Linda tomorrow."

A breeze picks up, from over the water. He returns my smile and his dimples show, under the man-not-boy five o'clock shadow on his face. God, he's good looking. "We've Only Just Begun" plays in my mind, the prettiest song I've ever heard. I don't tell Chuck, because it's a wedding song.

VERONA

After vacuuming perfect rows in the new wall-to-wall carpet, I admire my re-decorated living room and feel just one little spark of happiness. I'm trying, that's all I can say. A new look for a new start. No more army green and burnt orange here.

My living room and dining area are newly done in the Spanish style: red carpet, dark furniture and wrought iron accents.

Like Marty said, there is an upside to not having kids. I know he's just trying to keep what happened before from happening again and bless him for it. And he is right. After all, having a nervous breakdown over not getting what you want ain't appreciative of the many blessings one does have. If we'd had a child in the usual course of things, I'd have been at home instead of bringing in a decent salary for two whole decades. We wouldn't have this new carpet and furniture, or our other nice things.

We're even thinking about travelling now. Marty brought home a stack of brochures from the travel agency. He's got them fanned out all fancy on the new coffee table. We look through them together in the evenings.

I'd still trade everything in a New York minute for the patter of tiny feet around here, though. I suppose it's just a basic instinct that some of us ladies have, that stays with us and that's that. "Those carpet rows are so purty I hate to walk across them," Marty says, then tromps right through them, making a beeline for the big bowl of candy I fixed for the trick-or-treaters.

"Quit eating the 7-Up bars! I swan. Here, have you some candy corn. Did you get me them dimes for if we run out of candy? And we will run out, if you keep eating it all." I speak sharper than I mean to. But he deserves it, for that open bottle of beer he stashed behind a couch pillow when I came in.

He pulls a roll of dimes out of his pocket.

"I went by Venice's again after work," I say, deciding to ignore the beer incident. However, I am a firm believer that alcohol is a tool used by Satan to weaken and control the mind. And I'd respectfully invite anyone who takes issue with that to simply open their doggone eyes and look around them. How much emptier would the jails, the hospitals, and the orphanages be, if it wasn't for liquor?

"Any news?" he says, jolting me out of my thoughts.

"No news."

"You knocked on her door again?"

"I did. No answer. They've run off. Not a care in the world about me and you, neither, after all we done for them. I'm about fed up. But do you think they're okay, really? Tell me the truth, now."

"Oh sure," he says, for the hundredth time. "But it's been a while now. We need to go in the shack and have a look around. I'll go tomorrow. Just give me the key."

"No. That place is evil anyway and this is the worst time of the year for it."

"Honey, we can't have family missing and not check out whatever we can. Unless you've changed your mind about calling the law."

"Oh Marty, we've been through all this. Besides the embarrassment of having our family mess made public, you know there's a good chance Venice will have drugs on her or something She'd get locked up. Or Jaci would, for truancy. And then, in the end, they'd just come out even worse."

"I didn't come out worse."

"That's completely different. You didn't belong there in the first place. Oh, I don't know, Marty. It's such a doggone strange situation."

"It would be a strange situation for anyone but your crazy sister. But she does more strange things than she does normal things."

I open my mouth to tell him not to call my sister crazy, then change my mind. I've got a mind to wash my hands of Venice, after I find Jaci. I've started to think of Venice the same way I think of the ghost aunties, someone to stay away from. She's unholy, dangerous.

Marty says, "Look, it only makes sense to go in there. We might learn more about what's going on." He unwraps a miniature Snickers bar and pops it into his mouth, as if that settles the matter.

"Oh, all right," I say. I had actually already looked all over our house and found the spare key to Venice's house. Well, actually, to Venice's and my house, legally speaking. I start to hand it to him, then change my mind. I say, "I'll do it."

His eyes widen. I haven't set foot in that place in twenty years.

I had forgotten all about supper. I go to the kitchen to grab a couple of TV dinners from the freezer. I hope the neighbors won't see us from the doorway, when they bring their kids to trick or treat, eating such an embarrassing excuse of a dinner.

I'm putting the TV dinners in the oven when Marty says, like it's all a big joke, "Now, these so-called ghosts. Why are they all aunties? Where are the ghost unkies? Hey, you know, I never thought of that before."

If only he knew all I'd gone through to keep him from having to know how very real the ghost aunties are. People don't handle that kind of knowledge well. I don't even handle it well, and I was raised up with it. I say, "I don't know why there ain't no ghost uncles. I ain't in charge of the whole world, you know."

"Well, that *is* surprising to learn," he says, still thinking he is being a hoot.

The ghost aunties are not a topic I care to be mocked about. They are my blood relatives, some of who I loved very much, when they were on this side of the air curtain.

He says, "With your feelings on ghosts, I'm surprised you keep giving out candy every Halloween."

I swan, if that man don't get off the topic of ghosts... "Oh, stop. Costumes and candy is just good fun."

Mercifully, a knock comes at the door. I adjust my Minnie Mouse cap with the ears and big red polka-dot bow. The bowl full of the candy I bought for everyone else's children is so big I have to carry it with both of my white-gloved hands.

I unlock the door and step into the fortune-telling parlor, clutching my big cross pendant. It's like a dream, like stepping into a time warp portal in a science fiction picture show. The parlor looks about the same as I remembered. There's the same tall counter with the two barstools, the antique table with its two flowery upholstered chairs, the upholstery worn thin now, and the shelves, loaded down with creepy junk.

The burned section of windowsill is new. Jaci told Marty and I about it last spring. Someone had left a crystal ball on the windowsill, and sunlight coming through the window was concentrated through the crystal ball, until a small fire broke out. It made sense, when Marty said it's the same idea as how you can start a fire with a magnifying glass.

"Anybody home?" I call through the curtain, my voice shaking. When nobody answers, I step in.

In the kitchen, the refrigerator door hangs open. Its interior is clean and empty. I flip a switch but no light comes on. The food pantry is pretty bare but the cookware and plates are here.

The bedrooms and bathroom look fairly well cleared out, too. I exhale, realizing that my worst fear has not come about. That, of course, was that I'd find Venice and Jaci in here, dead.

It looks like what Marty and I have figured all along. Venice probably met a man, and they moved in with him. They didn't need most of their household stuff because he'd already have all that. Then, they didn't call me because they figured, correctly, that I would pitch a fit.

A skittering sound sends an icy sensation crawling up my back. I clutch my cross. A mouse darts across the floor.

I rush out the door, heart thumping. I'm not sure if I hear laughter or just imagine it.

VENICE

Every time I call Boring Barbara, she answers the phone the same way, all proper and shit. "Hello. Mrs. Miller speaking," she says. I picture Beaver Cleaver's mama, in an apron and pearls. Beaver Cleaver's mama is even named Barbara too, in real life. Barbara Billingsley. I wonder how Boring Barbara will answer the phone after the divorce is final. Mrs. Miller, still? Miss Whatever-her-maiden-name-is? Or maybe just "Hello. Boring Barbara speaking." Haha.

Sometimes their pudgy, pizza-face kid answers. He's a couple years older than Jaci. He says, "Hello, Miller residence. Richard Junior speaking. May I help you?"

In response to my silences, they both always say, "Hello?" exactly twice, before hanging up. I want to shush them because I'm trying to listen for Dick in the background. I'm listening for clues about where he's gone.

I'm still hanging on to hope that I'll be able to go back home as somebody better, a respectably married woman with a fine home, ready to hold my head up. I'd be in a position to suggest just leaving the past in the past. As I tell myself every day, it wouldn't be the first time Dick pulled a disappearing act, then came back to me. It makes me sick at my stomach to think of slinking home, tail between my legs, with no excuse nor nothing gained. I ran out on my *kid*. It may be the worst thing I've ever done. I mean, of course I knew Verona would handle it, or I never would of gone, but still.

I take a swig of bourbon from the bottle, then light a cigarette and go down the hall to fill my ice bucket. Right now, I just need to calm down and have a proper drink out of a glass, like a dignified individual. I ain't felt this goddamn low since I was pregnant with Jaci. And let me tell you, being a pregnant, unmarried teenager in 1960 was a whole lot worse than it would be today.

And that's before you even consider the rest of it.

I was so goddamned relieved at Jaci's features and coloring when she was born that I vowed to never ask for another goddamn thing for the rest of my life. So maybe that's it. Maybe I already used up my lucky break allowance in life and simply don't have no more coming to me.

I had got up my nerve to join in on a baseball game with a friend from school way back then, over at the park, the kind where anybody who wanted to could play. I wasn't showing much at all yet and figured I could get by with it. One last hurrah, I guess you could call it.

My little friend and I figured her parents wouldn't let her hang out with me no more, when the news got out that I was in the family way. I'd made up a story for my friend, about a whirlwind romance and a fiancé in the army. She thought I was big stuff and I enjoyed the attention. What fifteen-year-old wouldn't wish she had a fiancé who was in the United States Army? Even back then, I wasn't stupid enough to tell the full story, not to a soul.

I knew I wouldn't be allowed to go to school no more, not in those days. Mama and Verona had just caught on and they had a huge fight about it. Even then, Verona wouldn't come inside the shack, so Mama had to go out to the driveway to talk to her, and then Verona drove off in a huff, sending a big white dust cloud down the oyster shell driveway. That's the only time I ever heard Verona talk back to our mama in my whole life.

So I went off with my friend to go play ball in the park, just wanting to get my mind off the whole catastrophe for a little while. Nobody would believe this, these days, but the truth was that I wasn't even sure how I'd gotten pregnant. Oh, it was just a gigantic disaster. Doom with a capital D.

Anyway, today we had a bunch of people at the park, including a bunch of grown-ups, with picnic blankets and coolers full of beer and sandwiches.

About halfway through the game, I hit a home run! I had just passed first base when I heard a chant start up, with people clapping along to it. It seemed like everybody there joined in, from the other players to the spectators. I didn't understand that the chanting was meant for me until I made it to home plate and heard more chanting, louder, instead of congratulations for making it to home plate.

Then I made out the words: "Big fat pig! Big fat pig! Oink-oink!" *Clap-clap.* It got louder and louder as I ran around the bases. "Big fat pig! Big fat pig! Oink-oink!" *Clap-clap.* When the meaning of it finally dawned on me, I ran all the way home, practically on fire with shame. I felt like I'd been hit with a bomb, slammed with so much pure hatred from so many people all at once. That whole sticks and stones saying is wrong. Words can hurt you like a fucking bat upside the head, so bad you might never fully recover.

I ran home, and stayed home for six whole months. Mama and Verona heard about the incident at the ballpark and they said that was enough, that I wasn't going nowhere else. I didn't speak to another soul besides Mama, Verona and the ghost aunties, until Jaci was a couple months old. I only saw Verona out on the deck. She'd starting come up on the deck because she and Mama didn't want anyone seeing me in the driveway, in my condition.

When Mama's customers came to the fortune-telling parlor, I had to go stay in my room. At that time, Mama and Verona thought I would just go back to school like nothing had ever happened, after Jaci was born and put up for adoption. That's what they thought, even though I told them and told them I was keeping my baby. I could feel my baby kicking and moving. I created it, I grew it. It was mine. It was me. I couldn't give my baby away any more than I'd give my own stomach away.

I thought Mama and Verona would be really mad because I was pregnant but they were real nice to me. They treated me like I had the flu or a broken leg and required special attention.

Even the aunties were nice. Well, the aunties always was nice to children but I didn't think I qualified as a child no more.

Verona talked to me about the ugliness that went on at the park, after I kept having nightmares from it. She said the whole world didn't't really hate me, I was just a stand-in for their own fears. I ought to tell her sometime, how much that meant to me. She said she didn't understand why they were so mean either, until Marty explained it.

He'd said a pregnant girl with no boy around who could be assumed to be the daddy upsets the order of things. In

55

particular, it can strike terror in the hearts of the married women.

Verona said some of them women was no doubt worried that my baby's daddy was their husband. Add a couple of beers to that mindset, and you're all set for a big blow up.

But that's like shooting someone in the dark without first even bothering to look at who you are shooting. I didn't want their ugly and ancient husbands and couldn't imagine why anyone would. But the way I was treated gave me a strong grudge against married women, a grudge I carry to this day, even now that I hope to become a married woman myself.

I go over to the motel bar with my tarot deck at a little after five, when Bud comes on duty. He lets me offer the customers readings, even though it's considered solicitation, which is against the rules. I hang around the bar, dance a little to the jukebox and drink the free sweet tea and bourbons that Bud slips me. I only do two readings all night. I only make four bucks total.

At the end of the night, I help Bud clean up and ask if he feels like going on another surveillance mission. He says he's up for it.

We take drinks with us in to-go cups. Sweet tea and bourbon for me, rum and Coke for Bud. We smoke a joint on the way and sing along to The Eagles.

The Miller residence, Boring Barbara's residence, is dark. The outside lights have always been on the other times we drove by here at night. The double garage door is up and I can see by the streetlights that it's empty. The garage door has always been shut before.

Bud thinks this is strange, too. I mean, it's three in the fucking morning. He says, "What the hell?"

I say, "I'll be right back," and I open my car door, because I'm drunk and stoned.

Bud seems to have read my mind. He says, "Hold on a sec." I shut my door and we park a couple of houses up the street, then walk back to the Miller residence together. He leads the way into the garage.

The door from the garage to the house is locked. Bud pulls out his driver's license, wiggles it around between the door and its frame and pops the lock. I suddenly feel more sober. I suddenly feel great respect for Bud, for his loyalty and skills.

We step inside. I head for the stairs but Bud pulls me in a different direction. He knows what I'm after. He leads me to the master bedroom, which is here on the first floor.

I feel around for the wall switch and turn on the light, but Bud turns it off. "No, the bathroom light," he says. I get his point. There's less light that might be seen from the street that way.

Half the closet is full of women's clothes, shoes and purses. The other half is completely empty.

Bud says, "Satisfied?"

I say "Yes." I've just come to my senses and I want the fuck out of here, now. He turns the bathroom light off and we hurry out of the house.

Once we're safely back in Bud's car, I act like I wasn't just scared out of my goddamn mind. Bud and I agree that we're pretty much Bonnie and Clyde. We drive around the block and park in the nearby cul-de-sac, where we can keep the Miller residence under surveillance without being too obvious about it.

A car pulls into the Miller driveway and continues on, into the garage. A big woman gets out and pulls down the garage door. A couple minutes later, the outside lights come on. It looks like the show's over, so we leave. On the drive home, we discuss the situation.

Bud's theory is that one of them had some kind of medical emergency, most likely little Dick, since Boring Barbara was the one who got out of the car and shut the garage door. Under Bud's theory, they went to the emergency room at the hospital, in too much of a hurry to shut the garage door. Furthermore, he states, this emergency happened when it was still light out, which is why the outside lights weren't turned on.

I stand by my position that the two of them simply went zooming around town in the middle of the night, in a desperate and loony search for pie and ice cream. They went all crazy and caused everybody this much worry just because they're gluttonous fatties. They just can't help theirselves.

Bud says, "Meow!"

When he drops me off at the motel, I invite him to my room for a nightcap and one thing leads to another.

Later, with Bud snoring away next to me, I chain-smoke and try to figure out what it means that Dick's clothes ain't in that closet. He ain't there, and he ain't here. So where the fuck is he?

JACI

I'm worn out, after spending the day moving to Linda's. But I ought to cook supper anyway, to show my appreciation. "Y'all want Chef-Boy-ar-dee Ravioli? I got some canned green beans and some apple sauce too," I say, pulling cans out of the cabinets that I'd just finished putting into the cabinets. I'll have to clean up this nasty kitchen first, to even have enough room to cook or clean cookware to use.

Chuck says, "Great. Thanks, babe," cracking open a beer.

"What is that on your head? Did you bleach that white streak in your hair on purpose?" Linda says to me, with a tone that makes it sound like the real question is more like, "Are you an idiot?"

Chuck says, "Naw, she just has a spot on top of her head where her hair grows in white. t's natural."

"That's weird," Linda says. "Skunk woman!"

The two of them laugh, then go into the living room to watch TV and drink beer.

How rude. I clamp my mouth shut. I won't share this with Linda after her rude remarks but when I was little, the doctor told MeeMaw Jo that the white patch of hair was called a "poliosis." Supposedly, MeeMaw Jo got extremely upset because she thought the doctor was telling her that I had "polio."

The grown-ups always dyed the white streak, to blend in with the rest of my hair. I haven't gotten around to trying to dye it myself.

An hour later, exhausted, I go into the living room to announce that supper's ready but I stop when I hear them talking. Linda says, "No, a blow job is like third base. Definitely less dirty than fucking. Fucking is fourth base."

"No way," Chuck says. "I mean, you're putting it in your *mouth*. It's much dirtier than fucking, no doubt."

I stop, stunned. I would never talk to another girl's boyfriend like that. Chuck surely knows better, too. I'm already starting to think moving in here was a big mistake. I don't even feel like I can say anything back to Linda because, at this point, I'm just a nonpaying guest in her home.

I fix myself a plate and take it into my and Chuck's bedroom, without a word to either of them. Amara follows me down the hall. I say, "You can come in, sweetie." I feed her bites from my plate, feeling like she's the only friend I've got in the whole world.

VERONA

Nothing's changed at Venice's place. After getting home, I put the takeout burgers and fries on dinner plates. My life has gotten so much easier since McDonald's came to town. I pour myself a glass of Coke on ice and one for Marty too, pretending not to see the bottle of beer he stashed behind a sofa pillow again. I'm gonna be really mad if one of them beers spills on my new couch. I ask him to say grace. Maybe that'll nudge his tiny conscience.

I don't have an appetite because I'm upset. I say, "Another little one come up for adoption today. He's four years old, so they're looking at the second-choice couples for him." It's never officially stated, but everybody knows the County reserves any perfect White newborns that come its way for the first-choice couples on the waiting list. Married couples, not too young nor too old, with college educated fathers and stay-at-home mothers. Poorer, older or darker couples are only offered the children who are harder to place.

Marty says, "Oh, honey. I'm sorry."

"Oh, don't be. It just got to me today, that's all. The poor little thing was cute as a button, in his little overalls. He looked just like Dennis the Menace."

"Well, if he's anything like Dennis the Menace, you should be glad we can't have him."

Marty's joke fell flat with me. Marty and I would not be considered for any child at all through the County, because of Marty's criminal record. A private adoption was our only chance.

The adoption that recently fell through was the second time we'd gotten as far as going to the hospital to pick up a baby. Once, years ago, it was for a newborn girl. That time, we were told at the reception desk that the baby's teenage parents had decided to get married and keep the baby, after all. A few years after that, we worked with a divorced woman in Dallas, by phone and through the mail. The woman said she already had two children and couldn't handle another one.

Relieved to deal with an adult who knew her own mind this time, we paid the woman's living expenses for months. Then the due date came and went and the woman simply stopped answering our calls and letters. It was like she just dropped off the face of the earth.

Long story short, I fell apart. I don't even want to think about it. I even had to be hospitalized, briefly. As the doctor instructed, Marty packed up the baby things and put them out of sight before I returned home. He put them in the attic. From then on, we called the former nursery "the guest room."

There were other attempts that didn't make it as far as those three. But the baby issue is always there. I'm always waiting. In a way, I feel like I've been expecting for twenty years.

VENICE

The maid knocks on the door, even though I leave the "do not disturb" on the outside doorknob at all times. She keeps knocking and shouting, "Housekeeping! Housekeeping!" like it's a goddamn emergency. I just ignore her. She'll have to go away sooner or later. But then she has the nerve to put a key in the door and open it. The chain lock is on though, so she's only able to open the door a few inches.

I say, "Hello! Jenson residence. Venice speaking. May I help you?" I've had a couple drinks so I think that's pretty funny, although it is a private joke.

She finally goes away, thank goddamn god. But then the phone rings and it's the fucking manager, who informs me that I was supposed to have been gone by 11 a.m., which was three hours ago. He says, quite rudely I might add, that I need to pay up or get out or he will call the police! So then. Dick has stopped paying for the room.

I can't think of what to do, so I call Bud. I can't stay at his place because his girlfriend still lives there, though he always talks about making her leave. I guess I'm just always the bridesmaid, never the bride, or however the saying goes. But maybe Bud will have an idea or, better yet, pay for another night or two here, to give me a chance to figure out my next move.

Bud's unloved girlfriend answers the phone, like this: "What!" It's like she wants to fight whoever's on the other end, without even knowing who it is or anything. Her weirdly aggressive attitude cracks me up.

I say, "Hello! This is Barbara Boring Miller, manager of the Starlight Motel Bar? I'm calling to see if Budweiser can come into work a little early today." I call him "Budweiser" just to see what she'll do.

"Budweiser! Phone!" She screeches, right in my ear. Then she clunks the receiver down, on a hard surface.

When Bud comes to the phone, I tell him my predicament. He says, "I'll be right there." Long story short,

I'm still here. But I have a different room now, a smaller, shabbier one at the back end of the motel. I get it for free but it comes with various offers of work, which I am paid for, but expected to accept. I work wherever and whenever extra hands are needed throughout the motel complex, whether at the motel, bar, restaurant or washateria. My room is near the outdoor picnic table area.

The picnic table area is rented out now and then for outdoor parties. But mostly, it's a hangout for employees and regulars, like some of the truckers who come through here all the time and the regulars at the Starlight Bar. There's plenty of partying out here but I pretty much stayed away from it when I was with Dick. He thought the people were trashy.

Now this would be a set-up to be grateful for, if you didn't have nothing else going for you. But to me, it makes the ending of my hopes seem final, like Dick and I are definitely history. It's fucking terrible, as bad as if somebody died. My musty, ratty little room and life, compared to my scrapbook dreams.

JACI

A girl named Gail stops by Linda's trailer to see if we want to go hang out at the mall.

Me, Linda and Katie all jump at the chance. Usually, the only vehicle around here is Chuck's motorcycle, and he don't like shopping anyway.

Chuck says he'll stay home.

"Oh, come on. It's something to do," Linda says.

I brush Amara's hair, aggravated. I don't want Chuck there, trying to cut the trip short because he's bored, or trying to limit what I buy. I earn my way by watching Amara, not to mention doing most of the cleaning, cooking, grocery shopping and laundry, too. And I make a few bucks doing readings and selling some of the merchandise from the fortune-telling parlor.

It's my money, not his. I want to enjoy the mall without Chuck ruining it.

I say, "Which pretty barrettes do you want, Mar Mar? Do you want the blue bows? Or the

pink butterflies?"

Amara snatches the little plastic butterflies and I clip them into her fine yellow-white baby hair.

"There's no room for me in the car." Chuck says.

Linda says, "We'll find a way to fit everybody in. Come on. Please?"

I say, "Gail, is there room in your trunk for Amara's stroller?"

Gail nods.

Katie shakes her head.

"What? You don't want me to bring the stroller?" I say to Katie, confused.

"Uh, no."

"What, then? You're over there looking like you're mad at me."

"I ain't mad. I just wonder why you're always taking care of Amara and Linda's always taking care of Chuck, that's all."

Linda says, "Katie likes to stir up shit. Want to go home and stay there, Katie?"

Katie looks down at her feet, silent. I feel for her, even if Katie kind of deserved it, this time. It's Linda's place, so Linda has the upper hand with both Katie and me, and she has no problem using it.

I'm happy when Chuck stays home.

After we get back from the mall, I cut the tags off my cool new peasant top, puka shell

necklace and Charlie perfume. I put everything away before Chuck sees it. Luckily, he's out on his motorcycle when we get back.

He don't come home until after midnight, and then he goes straight to our bedroom without saying nothing.

I'm having too much fun to care what his problem is. Gail's boyfriend Dan is playing his guitar and we're all singing along to "American Pie." I felt a mood shift when Chuck came home though, and not in a good way. It's like I'm off balance, and I ain't even drinking. Things between me and Chuck have changed.

Me and Katie grate cabbage and carrots into a big bowl to make slaw for the get-together. A bunch of us are meeting on the beach for volleyball, beer and grilled seafood: fresh caught flounder, shrimp and oysters.

Chuck mopes on the old couch. He's on his second beer already, trying to ease his hangover by getting drunk again. He don't want to go to the beach. He don't want me to go, either.

He's mad about some guy, though all I did was light the dude's cigarette last night. At first, I thought Chuck was mad because he finally noticed I snitched his Zippo lighter. But no, he was mad because I lit the guy's cigarette, when the guy asked me to. According to Chuck, I should have just handed the guy the lighter, not flicked it for him.

I do secretly think a couple of the dudes that hang around Linda's are foxes but the guy in question ain't even one of them.

Katie says, "I hear you flicked some guy."

"I did, magpie. He was a great flick."

The kitchen is partly separated from the living room by a half-wall, so it's easy to forget that people in the living room might be able to hear you. Chuck hears us.

"Fuck you," he yells, then stomps to our bedroom and slams the door.

Katie mutters, "No, flick *you*."

"Guess I better go talk to the flickhead," I say, wiping my hands on a dish towel. I'm super aggravated now/

Chuck slamming the bedroom door woke Amara from her nap and she comes out of her room, crying. I get her settled on the living room rug, with a stack of blocks and a sugar cookie, and then I have to use the restroom.

By the time I get to our bedroom, Linda's already there, kneeling by the bed and talking all sweet to Chuck, who is a fussy baby like Amara, only nowhere near as cute. I almost ask him if he wants a damn cookie too, but I don't want to give Linda any ammunition. She just loves to jump in on Chuck's side whenever Chuck and I have a disagreement.

Instead, I announce, all chipper-like, "Well, I have to change clothes now."

Linda takes a hint for once and leaves the room. I shut and lock the door after her. Chuck's tear-streaked face icks me out.

He yelled at me for two hours straight late last night, then he smacked my face. It wasn't a hard slap, but I still feel like I hate him for it. He didn't apologize for waking Amara just now, either.

I blurt out, "Crybaby." I'm sorry as soon as I say it because I know it is gonna be a Big Thing.

Baby Chuck covers his face with the pillow. I apologize. I lay down next to him and rub his back, clenching my teeth the whole time.

He finally takes the pillow off his face. I keep talking nice to him. He is such a drag. I can't wait get to the beach party. I hope Chuck stays home.

Linda went to work, so that's one drag out of the way. The trailer's living room is crowded. It's me and Amara, Chuck, Katie, Gail and Gail's boyfriend Dan, with his guitar again.

A few other people come and go throughout the night.

We take up a collection for pizza. Someone goes to get it. Then the guy who'd wanted a light from me shows up. He sits on the floor, right next to me, dangit, and starts singing along with everybody else. Gail's boyfriend plays "Sweet Home Alabama."

I sing and clap Amara's hands with mine. On the other side of me, Chuck's getting agitated. He keeps setting his beer down, then picking it up again and balling up the fist of his beer-free hand. I look around the room but there's really no place to move to that wouldn't be awkward.

The song ends. The guy puts a cigarette in his mouth and turns to me. "Got a light?" he says.

Chuck starts weirdly blinking.

I can just see Mama now, holding her finger up like she's making an announcement and saying, "SNAFU." She'd have that hilarious, exaggerated look on her face.

I pick up the Zippo and hand it to the guy, without looking at him.

I don't even want it back. I take Amara into her room, to the rocking chair, though it's a little early for her bedtime. I sing along with the guitar.

I think the guy who wanted the light actually has his eye on Katie. I consider telling Katie but decide to drop it, since the guy makes Chuck crazy, just by existing.

I put Amara, asleep now, into her crib, then go to bed myself. I'm thinking about breaking up with Chuck.

I don't know what went wrong. I've been waiting for Chuck to be Chuck again but it's like he's turned into somebody else. He gets so drunk he ruins the fun. He'll shout the same thing over and over again, like "Led Zeppelin, man! Led Zeppelin," eight hundred times. And he throws tantrums. He's moody and he cries to get sympathy. Once, he even wet the bed.

I hate to even think this since I'm just sick about Mama going missing, but Chuck reminds me of her now. It's not romantic, when your boyfriend reminds you of your mama.

Chuck has a job for a couple of days, helping some big family move from one house to another in town. Linda is glad he's gone because she is stuck on the idea of throwing a huge birthday party for him, and she's stuck on it being a surprise. It seems strange to me. Chuck don't even know that many people here, for one thing. But I'm getting into it, learning how to put together a big bash. It's a super cool thing to be able to do. And this is a safe way to learn it. I ain't the main organizer, so if nobody shows up, I won't be the one who looks like the world's least popular jack-ass.

Linda, Katie and I walk over to the grocery store to buy the party food. Linda don't seem to have a single worry in her head about if the party's a flop. I kind of hope it does flop, just so her ass gets taken down a peg. I pull Amara along, in a red wagon with tall wooden sides.

We'd put out word of Chuck's birthday bash to our school friends and Linda's co-workers at the Blue Moon Bar. Linda's having a keg delivered from there.

We fill two shopping carts with packs of hot dogs and buns, ketchup, mustard, and economy-size containers of cold beans and potato salad. We all agreed on the shopping list and we agreed to keep it simple. This way, hopefully, the money we collect from the guests will cover the cost of the party. But now Linda won't stop talking about birthday cake. "I wonder if he likes chocolate?" she says for the third time, studying a Betty Crocker mix.

Katie says, "Cake ain't on the list."

"Don't worry about it, dumbo. I'll cover the cost if we don't get enough back."

I think of a story Chuck had told me, about some older friend of his in Ohio, a biker.

Some chick sat on this biker's Harley without the biker's girlfriend's permission. Chuck said that is a big no-no. The girlfriend was so mad about the disrespect that she pulled the other girl's top clear off her, pulled it right off over the girl's head, somehow. Then she pulled the topless girl off the bike and whooped her. I laughed my head off when Chuck acted the scene out, complete with all the shrieking and flopping.

Linda's interest in Chuck's birthday is that same type of violation but I can't muster up the enthusiasm to yank Linda's top off her in the cake mix aisle. The most payback I can bother with is just not telling her that Chuck don't really like chocolate.

I bounce Amara on my hip as our little group goes through the store. "Bouncy-bouncy bounce. Hey, looky over there! Does Mar Mar want to pick out a big bouncy ball to take home?" Mar Mar certainly does. She's so precious, so seriously pointing her chubby finger at the green ball, then the yellow one. She finally settles on a pink ball, which is no surprise to me.

On the walk home, the wagon is full of groceries and we had to borrow a shopping cart, too. Amara carries the big ball I bought for her, and I carry Amara.

The next day, Saturday, we clean house, fix food and get ourselves dolled up. Finally, we lounge in the living room, taking a break before the party starts.

"It looks like a brand-new place, with the windows washed," Katie says. Outside, branches and logs are stacked by the fire area. "Y'all sure it ain't too hot out for a fire?"

"Duh, it's autumn," Linda says. "And did you forget about them beach fires all summer long anyhow, airhead?"

More of Linda's digs. Me and Katie exchange a look.

"What are you looking at?" Linda says.

"Me? Nothing," I say.

Linda says, "Can I ask you something?"

"I guess."

"Don't take this the wrong way. But are you part Black? You kind of look it, you know."

Katie gasps. This is going too far, even for Linda.

I keep my voice low and slow when Linda starts with her reminders that she's top dog.

I act like I don't really even notice her that much. I say, "My daddy was Portuguese."

Linda says, "Hmm," which you could take to mean agreement, or not.

"Where's Mar Mar?" I say, louder than I mean to, covering Amara's eyes with my hands. Then I remove my hands from her face. I shout, "Peek-a-boo!" She falls down, giggling.

Me and Katie try to ignore Linda's rude moods because if Linda gets mad enough, Katie will lose her place to get away from her folks and I'll lose my place to live. And I won't get to see Amara anymore. Katie and I probably wouldn't get to hang out with the cool older crowd anymore, either.

Small paper plates, with frosted chocolate cake squares, cover the kitchen table. Linda straightens the display.

She says, "I hope Chuck likes his cake." Me and Katie exchange another look.

Amara holds out her chubby arms. I stub out my long Salem, then pick her up. I bounce her on my knee. "How does the horsie go, Mar Mar? Horsie goes neigh! Horsie goes bouncy bounce!"

"Ball goes bounce!" she says.

I say, only sort of kidding, "Oh my god. Did you hear that? She might be a genius, y'all." The party guests start showing up. We've put on "I'm Eighteen" by Alice Cooper, which we plan to keep playing over and over again while the party gets started.

We draw a star on each guest's right hand with a purple marker, after they pay their two-dollar entry fee.

A while later, I'm in Amara's room, trying to rock her to sleep, in spite of all the party noise. I'm already partied out, to be honest. I like smaller get-togethers a lot better, a few people singing along to Gail's boyfriend's guitar, or a half dozen people just sitting around talking or playing cards. Big, loud parties are too much. I only realized this at the beach party the other day.

Even though I couldn't wait to get there, I felt like leaving right away. So, I missed it when Linda's manager offered Chuck a bartending job at the Blue Moon Bar, now that he's old enough to serve liquor. And I missed it when Chuck opened a gift from Linda, a pocket watch, engraved with his initials.

I didn't get him anything. I'd thought chipping in for the party would be enough.

When I finally get my period, I can't stop chanting "thank god, oh thank god," in my mind, even though the only supernatural beings that I know for sure exist are the ghost aunties. And I don't even want to think about how high and mighty they'd get, if they ever got wind of anyone sending divine thanks to them. Not to mention all the godawful noise they'd make if they knew I'd had sex. At the shack, I always slept with a row of pillows in the bed between me and Chuck, to keep the aunties quiet. I passed it off to Chuck as me just being shy and wanting to take things slow.

The past week had me wishing I'd stuck with that row of pillows after moving into Linda's place. It's been a dang nightmare, all that worry. I don't see what the big deal is about sex anyway. Especially at the end, when he's huffing and puffing like the little engine that could.

I want to shout, "All aboard!" Or maybe just "I am bored." Anyhow, that's it. My sex life is over. It ain't worth all this, that's for damn sure.

Amara cries in her crib, so I go in to check on her. She feels hot. I pick her up and head for the kitchen. I remember seeing a bottle of baby aspirin in the junk drawer there.

When I turn on the living room light, Chuck and Linda jump up from the sofa. They were lying there, together.

I jump, too. I didn't know anybody was out here. They scared me to death. Amara shrieks, also startled.

"Uh," Chuck says. "Uh."

I get a strange sensation like I'm levitating, like when Mary Poppins soared up to the sky with her umbrella.

Then my mind slowly floats back down into my body, and it's calm and clear. I mean, ain't this just right? Chuck with Linda. And me with Amara.

Amara starts whimpering. I say, "Um, she feels hot." I carry Amara to the kitchen and coax her into chewing up the little orange flavored tablets. I fix a cold, wet washcloth for her too, and fill a sippy cup with apple juice.

Chuck is standing up, when we come back into the living room. He says, "It's not how. We were just. I can. Let's talk. Babe."

His words seem out of place. He already looks like some guy from my past. I realize now, that's how I had come to see him, even before this. What I feel, just below the confusion, is relief. He and I are finished, and I'm relieved.

I say, "Say night-night, Mar Mar. Nighty-night!"

Amara says, "Nigh nigh," and I flip the light switch off again, putting Chuck and Linda back into darkness.

I hold Amara in the rocking chair, awed by her sweetness. The pudgy cheeks, the rosebud mouth. I would love to be a real mother. But I just do not understand how something as big as a newborn baby, bigger than a five-pound bag of sugar, could make its way into the world without splitting its mother in half. You'd have to be out of your dang mind to want that.

I rock Amara for a while more after she falls asleep. A plan forms in my mind.

VERONA

Marty was worried that I'd have another breakdown. I was fighting it pretty good but it snuck up on me anyway and I did start to feel pretty low, a lot of the time. He'd call me at work to ask how I feel. He started going to church with me, which he hardly ever used to do. He was looking a little haggard himself. We were getting to be like one big dog, chasing its own tail. I knew it didn't help nobody to dwell and mope about what I can't have. I saw what Marty was getting at, with them travel brochures.

But neither of us had even been out of Texas. We finally admitted that a foreign country, an ocean cruise or even an airplane flight just seemed like too much of a stretch. Then, a gal at church happened to be telling everyone about her recent trip to San Antonio. After hearing her excitement about it, Marty and I looked at each other like, that's it!

Oh, my goodness! There was so much to do and see, and only a half day's drive away. I got a pan of homemade enchiladas in the oven right now. Marty just went to pick up our photos, and we plan to have a nice Tex-Mex dinner while we reminisce about our trip.

Marty's favorite thing was the Alamo. Mine was, of all things, the cave with the artifacts and all the bats in it. I also enjoyed quite a bit of shopping. Fortunately, the Mexican handicrafts look pretty doggone good with my new Spanish décor. After all, the two countries do have shared history.

I bought some Mexican pottery, a handwoven couch throw, a cute Mexican dress, leather sandals and some silver jewelry. I bought a few things for Jaci and put them in her bedroom here.

I like to picture the expression that will be on her face when she comes home and finds her presents.

We were sitting on a bench to take a break, in front of a little Mexican pottery shop that we'd just shopped in, when a stray kitten came up to Marty, mewling and rubbing against his leg.

Well, guess who came home with us? She's got four different colors: black, orange, white and brown, all in patches. She reminded me of the colorful Talavera pottery inside the shop, so that's what we named her, Talavera. Forcing myself to get on with life don't end my worry about Jaci and Venice, of course, nor my sadness about the latest adoption fiasco. But it makes my sorrows more a part of my life, rather than my entire life.

VENICE

I get my hopes up when the phone rings. I doubt the office staff would give Dick the phone number to my new room. But I figure they'd call if anyone came around looking for me, since they know me now.

I have fifty percent accepted that Dick and I are through. Then again, sometimes we don't get along, which is a typical downside of highly passionate relationships. And then, a break is good for both of us, in a way. It is definitely still possible that this is just a break.

I answer the phone. It's only the head maid. She says, "Do you want to clean some rooms today? A couple of the girls called in sick."

"Sure. I'll be right there, hon."

The other maids are already at work when I get to the utility area. I load my cart with towels, sheets and soaps. I like cleaning rooms. There's satisfaction in bringing a mess into perfect order.

After stepping into the first room on my list, I pull the cart across the doorway, as instructed in my training, to help keep stray weirdos from wandering in.

In the bathroom, I wipe off the counter and lay out a line of white powder. Getting through eighteen or twenty rooms in one day is a lot. A snort or two helps. It clears my mind, too. The clean white powder goes up into my brain and sanitizes it of painful thoughts.

At lunchtime, I get a burger and fries to go, from the Starlight Motel restaurant. I'm too coked up to feel like eating right now but it's half price, an employee perk. I'll eat it later. I take it to the picnic area out back. I'm happy to see that someone has left a newspaper on one of the tables. I like the crossword puzzle.

"Hello there, beauty," Bud says.

"Oh, hey! I didn't see you over there. Know where I can get a pen, hon?"

"I'll get you one from the bar. Or would you rather do a line with me?"

"Why yes, Mr. Budweiser, I believe I would." He don't need to know I'm already flying.

I do a line, then he does a line. I do another line because I feel so goddamn good.

He says, "Whoa, gorgeous. Slow down there."

I smile fetchingly, so he'll quit being fucking stingy. I point at the tabletop. He shakes his head, but then he lays out another line for me.

Later, I hover above the picnic table, listening to the sirens come closer while people gather around. *Just wait until Dick hears about this.* I'm happy to think of how worried he'll be.

Venice was loaded into the ambulance and whisked away.

Bud was no fool so he was long gone from the picnic area by then but her lunch remained in its paper bag on the table, unopened. Before long, a sloppily groomed young man spotted it there and gobbled it up, his eyes darting about warily.

JACI

I don't leave until Linda and Chuck wake up. It should be all right to leave Amara here for a while, with both of them home.

On the walk to my and Mama's shack, I run through my mental list again. The nights get cold now, so I'll have to find both sleeping bags. I pass by a neighborhood where some of my

old school pals live. I feel like I'm in the wrong time period, like Rip Van Winkle. During Rip's twenty-year nap, the world changed around him but I have changed in the past few months, while the rest of the world seems to have stayed the same. My old English teacher would have liked that insight.

I'll need a can opener, matches, long pants, sweaters. This will take a few trips. The Gulf is flat and brownish gray today and so is the vegetation on the dunes. The island has died for the winter. When the shack comes into view, I feel sorry for it, left all alone. Maybe I am ditzy, like Chuck called me that time. Not that I care what Chuck thinks. Chuck, with that stupid way he blows air up to his bangs with his mouth, making his hair flutter on his forehead when he's mad.

In my bedroom, I spread a sleeping bag out on the floor, to be loaded up with other items. I hear a voice. "My girl."

I freeze.

Then I rush through the place, opening doors and closets, looking under the furniture. I say, "Mama? Mama, where are you?"

"Up here with the aunties, hon. I've gone beyond the curtain."

I bundle what I can carry into the sleeping bag and go out the door. When I reach the bay, I slosh through water up to my hips, the cold barely registering. I drop the bundle onto the floor of the elevated fishing shack, then go back the way I came.

I keep on going, automatic, like a machine.

Back at my and Mama's shack, I gather up another load, this time piling things into my laundry basket. Through the curtain made of air, Mama says, "Don't cry, baby. We're all just passing through."

I didn't know I was crying but I am.

Mama says, "I always meant to come back for you, you know."

"I'm so sorry for the way I spoke to you. I didn't ever, ever want you to die." There. At least I finally got a chance to tell her that.

She says, "I know, baby. Don't worry."

The aunties' patience breaks. The humming begins.

"Oh boo-hoo, hoo-boo. Boo!" one of them calls out.

"Stop spoiling the kid. She'll live."

"Or not!" A chorus of laughter follows.

The aunties get highly insulted when anyone acts like being dead - like they are - isn't every bit as good as being alive. As far as they're concerned, there's no more difference between being alive and dead than there is between, say, living on the island or on the mainland, just across the bridge.

Mama yells at them. "Hush up, you old gin jinns."

The humming grows louder.

"You haints ain't saints," Mama says, and hums back at them. Hearing the usual bickering makes me feel a tiny bit better.

After three trips to the fishing shack, I'm soaked, freezing and exhausted, on top of being totally gutted about Mama. I'll have to stop for the night now. I'll just have to hope everything will still be here when I can get back to it.

Back at the trailer, Amara is home alone, pulling pots and pans and cleaning supplies out of the bottom kitchen cabinets. If I had any small doubt about my plan before, I don't now.

VERONA

I went inside Venice's place again a couple of days ago. Right away, I noticed the cast iron skillet was gone from the stovetop. I'm sure it was there before. I remember thinking I'd use

it as a weapon if anybody came after me. A bath towel was gone, too. I remember its bright yellow color, and feeling it to see if it was damp the first time I went inside, checking to see if it had been recently used. It had been hanging over the shower curtain rod. So, Venice and Jaci must be staying nearby, close enough to come and get things from the shack as needed.

I have a couple of Avon deliveries to make out this way, so I'm just gonna pull into Venice's driveway real quick and check on the place from the outside, at least.

After I told Marty about the signs that they'd been in the shack lately, he warned me not to go in there anymore, just in case it wasn't them in there taking things. He got somebody to start helping us keep an eye on the place. It's the retired daddy of some young guy who Marty hired to help with his drywall business.

The old man parks on the side of Beach Drive, near where you'd turn off onto Venice's driveway. He's instructed to snap photos from the safety of the car, if he sees anyone, then drive to the nearest pay phone and call Marty. But he can only do it a few hours a day and it's only been a couple of days so far. It's something, anyhow.

One thing that's odd is that Venice didn't take her car. It's been there this whole time, parked crooked under the shack. But knowing Venice, it probably broke down and she just let it sit there.

Now... a window is busted out. And the window is open. It looks like someone went up on the deck, smashed the window out, then reached in and opened it from the inside, and climbed through it.

I'm flustered now. I back down the driveway fast and head for home. I can't even think clearly until I get on the bridge, off the island.

But, when you think about it, Venice could have broke in her doggone herself. She is prone to losing things. It could be she just lost her key and broke the window. She and her latest Prince Charming might be out buying new window glass right now, for all I know.

I forget about my Avon deliveries until I turn onto Crepe Myrtle Drive. I'll have to call my customers and tell them a white lie.

I barely make it through the door when the phone starts ringing. It's the hospital chaplain. He is calling to inform me that Venice is dead.

I must have screamed because Marty comes running out to the kitchen, saying, "What's wrong?" What's wrong?"

According to the chaplain, Venice was DOA at the emergency room. She'd had a heart attack, likely brought on by an overdose of cocaine.

I had Venice buried next to my parents, a quick decision and a quick end to the whole ordeal, physically at least. I declined to hold a public service or even put an obituary in *The Daily News*. I did not feel able to hold up to anyone's sympathy or questions. I could barely hold on to whatever marbles I had left as it was.

Now I feel that may have been a wrong decision, regardless of how I felt at the time. But most of all, I just want to find Jaci.

Marty pulls a long metal pole out of the back of his work van. "Just in case we need a weapon. But ninety-nine percent, nobody's in there. The old man ain't seen anybody come in or out, either." Then Marty says to me, louder, "What's with the boombox? Turn it off." I can tell he's nervous.

"If anybody *is* in there, I want them to hear us coming," I lie. The boombox is to drown out any noise from the aunties

"We don't need that," he yells, over the music.

I pretend like I don't hear him.

He shrugs and keeps walking. He knocks on the door. "Anybody home? Anybody home?" he says.

He opens the door. An odor wafts out. The fortune-telling parlor has been trashed. Some of the shelves have been knocked over, scattering books, candles and incense holders.

Marty calls through the curtain. "Anybody home? Anybody home?"

He motions for me to stay behind him. He enters the kitchen, his pole at the ready. The kitchen is ransacked, too. A syringe lays on the floor, like it was placed there for dramatic effect in a cheesy low-budget movie.

I pull up the bottom of my blouse and cover my nose and mouth with it. The stench is stronger here. The room seems to slowly swirl, as it hits me that Jaci could be in here, dead.

Marty checks the bedrooms, the closets and under the beds. The bathroom is horrifying.

It's been used, a lot, though the water's shut off. Marty says, "Okey-dokey. All clear. I'm just gonna board up the busted window real quick and then we'll go. You can wait in the van, if you want." He says it loud, to be heard over my boombox. He goes out the door. He's annoyed with me.

I feel sick at my stomach. This place always did bring on my stomach problems, even before this newest desecration. This place was originally built and used as a church, a holy place, a house of the Lord. That's enough of this doggone Satan's den. Enough.

Marty says, "Are you coming?"

"I'll be right there, dear."

He goes out to his truck to get the plywood and other supplies to board up the broken window. I carry out what had so far just been a recurring daydream of mine. I gather all the crystal balls I can carry, from the fortune-telling parlor shelves, the table and the floor, bundling them up in the bottom of my blouse.

I rush around the shack, placing crystal balls on the windowsills, throughout. I go back for more. Within minutes, multiple crystal balls line every windowsill in the place, aside from the one Marty is outside boarding up.

There are three to five crystal balls on each of the five windowsills. As an afterthought, I hurry back through the place one more time. I gather up papers, matchbooks, Kleenex and socks and place them around the crystal balls. I grab whatever catches fire easily.

I exhale, so long and deep I feel like I'd been holding my breath half my life. I make for the door. I turn off the boombox.

I hear the aunties:

We're going to be set free!

Thank the good Lord.

Endlich frie. Wunderbar!

It's about motherfucking time.

I recognize that last voice as Venice's. I whisper, "Good-bye, baby sister. Good-bye."

Marty's standing outside, a question on his face. "My stomach's acting up again," I say, and get in the van.

Yes. This will restore the natural order of things. It will finally be the way it was meant to be all along.

VENICE

A body is a harsh master, a crushing burden, a life sentence in a prison cell. A body is hot, or it's cold, hungry or in pain. It craves this and it needs that, incessant fucking demands that enslave the soul within.

Until it's gone. And then, you're free.

JACI

I sweep the one-room fishing shack, nail sheets up in the window cut-outs, and straighten the built-in ladder that serves as stairs. I make it as much a home as I can. It's on its own miniature island, a sand spit, I think it's called. I think it's pretty nice, when I get done. I wish I had somebody to show it off to.

The days fall into a rhythm. After getting myself and Amara up, dressed and fed, I dump out the water bucket and put it in the rowboat that I "borrowed" from a better, currently vacant, fishing shack. We row over to the Isla Ajaja, where we stroll the beach, like I did with Mama when I was little.

Amara attracts grandma-aged snowbirds like white on rice. Some of these older ladies go ga-ga over babies and small children. Sometimes one of them will come after us with a gleam in her eyes that's so eager it's kinda scary. They like little kids even better than the young mothers do. The young mothers are busy with their own children.

I make small talk with the grandmas and give them a chance to make friends with Amara before taking my small crystal ball out of my jacket pocket, and asking if they want a scrying for a buck. A lot of times they say yes. It's kind of lousy because I know they're just being nice, feeling sorry for me, a "young mother" who has to practically beg in public. It's a whole different thing from when customers choose to come into our fortune- telling parlor.

Mama mostly used tarot cards so I'm lots more used to them. With the crystal ball, sometimes I stumble through it and make dumb mistakes. But cards are a hassle on the beach, especially when it's windy.

The beach campground is full of retired people in motor homes and campers this time of year. I agree with Mama and Aunt Verona that they stopped driving too soon. It can get cold in the winter here. They ought to go down to south Florida or at least to South Padre Island. But if you were from somewhere arctic like Wisconsin or Minnesota, I guess you wouldn't know no better. Sometimes a lady snowbird will invite us to lunch.

On the way home, I always re-fill the water bucket, from the outside spigot of a vacant bay house. We stop in at the mini-mart if we need anything, then row back to our tiny island, where we stay until the next morning.

The snowbird grandmas think I'm twenty-two-year-old Staci Fox, wife of Drake Fox, who is really a character from one of Aunt Verona's Harlequin romance novels. I have red hair now, that I dyed myself, a silver wedding band and a little daughter named "Maureen."

After playing the role for a while, I almost start to believe it. I wish it was real. I say grown up things like, "Drake wants another kid but I told him not to even think about it until this one's in school." Or "Drake thinks we'll be able to buy a house next year."

I feel like I'm starring in an episode of *The Twilight Zone*, like I was snatched up out of my life and plopped down somewhere else, with no way back.

This must be how Chuck felt after he rode his motorcycle out of his life in Ohio. Now that I know how hard it is to start your whole life over alone, I feel like nobody would want to, at least not for very long. There must be more to that story.

Did he somehow get himself pushed out of his real life, too? Either way though, I still can't stand him.

We're at the camp of two retired sisters. I'm drinking coffee with them at the folding table they've set up under their travel trailer's awning. Amara is over at their cold fire grate, pretending to cook with some empty pots they brought out for her.

"What time you got there, ma'am?" I ask the sister who wears a watch.

"Let's see. It's 2:30."

I have just enough time to meet Katie at her bus stop. On an impulse, I decide to do it. I tell them I have to run. I pick up Amara and rush off.

When Katie steps off the school bus and sees us, she says, "Oh, magpie. What in the fucking hell have you done?"

I held my breath, until the ends of Katie's mouth turn up in a smile. When I feel sure she's still my friend, I say, "Come along, sex pervert. You, too, shall be snatched away from a life of shititude."

"It's about time," Katie says, bowing down in an exaggerated way, as if heavily burdened by her schoolbooks or her life.

"Here, I'll trade you," I say. I put Amara on Katie's back, then take Katie's books.

I say, "Show Aunt Katie how you can hold on like a big girl, Mar Mar."

"Horsie goes moo!" Amara says.

I say, "Magpie goes… What does a magpie say?"

"Magpie says where the fuck are you taking me?"

"Oh my, such language. You are a dirty, dirty bird. What does the dirty bird say, Amara? Ah, here we are. Ready to get in the boat, sex pervert?"

Once we reach the islet, I show Katie around. After the summer we had together, I consider her my very best friend. I have missed her.

Katie says, "Wow. This is nice."

"Thanks." I light a cigarette, not wanting to seem like a doofus who gets all excited about getting a compliment. I say, "Stay for supper." We're inside the fishing shack so I ask her to carry Amara down the little ladder. I follow, with a big can of ravioli and a can of green beans.

We make a fire and talk.

"Am I on Linda's shit list or what?" I say, all casual, like it don't make no difference to me, one way or the other.

Katie says, "I doubt it, knowing her."

"Yep. Oh, hold on, I forgot the applesauce."

Amara says, "Appasaw, Mama."

Katie says, "Mama? Really?" She's got a tone.

"Oh. Um, she just calls me that sometimes. I don't even know why," I lie, to try and get along. But what I'm really thinking is that I deserve to be called Amara's Mama because I'm the one who acts like Amara's Mama, dang it. I can't help but defend myself, even if in a roundabout way. I say, "You remember how Linda was with her, right?"

Katie nods. But when I come back with the applesauce, the mood is different. After a while, Katie says, "I should have been the one to take her. I'm family. You're not."

It pisses me off. I say, "Oh, I'm definitely her family now."

Katie's mouth tightens up, like it does when she's about to cry. Good. She deserves to cry. Bigmouth.

But then I feel kind of bad, even though she's got the nerve to try to claim a superior position over me, when I rescued this girl and have been the one taking care of her, round the clock, for weeks.

What's Katie done, besides happen to be related to crap-face, whore-head Linda? If anything, Katie should get a beating for that. That almost makes me laugh out loud.

But I didn't bring Katie here to fight with her. I take a deep breath and try to get back to the mood we started out with. I ask about Gail and Gail's boyfriend with the guitar. I ask about school, if Katie ever sees Miss Tampon, magpie extraordinaire. But Katie only gives me one-word answers.

As soon as she's through eating, she asks to go home.

I row her back across the bay, still trying to act like nothing's wrong. Back on the island, she climbs out of the boat. I hand her books to her. I say, "Say bye-bye to Aunt Katie, Mar Mar."

I say, "See ya, magpie."

But she just walks away.

VERONA

I settle in at my desk with a freshly filled mug and the newspaper. I like to ease into my workday with coffee and the crossword puzzle, before the others get here.

I'm not prepared for the full-page picture of the blazing shack, splashed across the front page of *The Daily News*. Hot coffee sloshes all over my desk.

Madame Venice's Fortune-Telling Parlor, a longstanding island tourist attraction, has burned down. The business had been closed for several weeks. It was vacant at the time of the blaze.

"Whoopsie! You got quite a puddle there." I didn't hear Betty Lou Thomason come in.

"It's okay. I have to get up anyway. I spilled some on my blouse."

But Betty Lou's already here with paper towels, wiping coffee off the desk. She sees the newspaper.

She says, "What's this? That fortune-telling parlor burned down?"

"Apparently so. Oh, well. With that nonsense gone, maybe more people will find their way to church."

"That's true. Say, wasn't that some relation of yours who ran that place?"

"I hope this coffee don't stain." I hurry to the kitchen part of the office and make myself busy at the sink, trying to run the coffee-splotched part of my blouse under the water, the best I can without taking it off. I'm waiting for Betty Lou to go to her desk.

But busybody Betty Lou follows me to the sink. She says, "My girls know Jaci. In fact, I believe Jaci was staying with my older daughter, Linda."

I spin around. "Is she there now?" I catch myself and start over, in my pleasant, conversational voice. I say, "Oh, really? Does your daughter live on the island?"

But a look passes between us, one that cuts through the pleasantries.

Betty Lou says, "I think we should talk."

I'm eager to hear more but the last thing I need is for anyone else to wander in and get an earful of my family's dirty laundry. So, I say, "Come over for dinner after work. I'll write down my address."

Betty Lou accepts my invitation. I try to think of what kind of shape I left the house in, and what I can whip up for dinner real quick this evening.

When I get home, I ask Marty to go away. He looks surprised and hurt, which is so cute I almost laugh. I slow myself down enough to explain that one of the gals from work is coming over to give me some information about Jaci. I say, "I reckon it will be less awkward if it's just us gals. She's likely to say more that way."

Let's face it, Jaci's a young girl running wild, without adult supervision. I expect to get a report on her that is less than a G, as the movie ratings go. I'm nervous about just *how* bad it might be, though. Hopefully PG-rated then, not R. Or, Lord have mercy, X. And Betty Lou's a bit from the old school, as far as what is discussed in mixed company.

Marty perks up about there being news about Jaci, at last. I get antsy though, when he takes his doggone time picking out a few magazines to take with him, from the end table shelf: Popular Mechanics, National Geographic and Reader's Digest.

I need to cancel some of them subscriptions. We don't get around to reading them and they just pile up and gather dust. He finally leaves for Brown's diner.

I zip around, straightening up the place. Then I start a supper of spaghetti with Ragu, frozen peas, frozen carrots, and cottage cheese with canned peaches. Mama always said you need a minimum of three side dishes for company. I don't want Betty Lou to have cause to go around saying I lack homemaking skills.

Jaci's been gone for five long, heart twisting months. I'm equal parts dread and excitement mixed up together, which equals a nervous stomach for me. I doubt I'll be eating much of the dinner I'm fixing.

Marty comes in as soon as Betty Lou leaves. I'm already in the guestroom with a pen and notebook. I didn't even stop to load the supper dishes into the dishwasher first. I'm making a list, splitting my attention between it and Marty. He says, "What the heck were you gals talking about that took so long?"

I stop to explain the entire situation to him. I swan, I didn't see *this* plot twist coming. Never would have imagined it in a million years. But, as they say, every cloud has a silver lining.

I talk while I write. "Let's see, we'll need a gallon of pink paint and a gallon of white, and some masking tape. I want to do the walls in pink and white stripes. Or should we get yellow instead of pink?"

"Honey…"

"Oh, and can you bring all that baby stuff down from the attic one day this week? We probably can't use most of it for a three-year-old, but we can sort through it anyhow."

"Honey. Let's not get our hopes up."

I look up from my notes and glare at him.

He sighs, in an unnecessarily exaggerated way. I decide to ignore it.

I say, "I think we can keep the dresser and double bed that's already here but I want a new bedspread for her. Maybe with a print like Holly Hobbie or something like that, but it would have to go with the walls. Maybe I'll sew one myself. Have you seen the tape measure?" I add to my list: *Bedspread* or fabric for bedspread (matching thread).

He leaves the room and comes back with the tape measure. He says, "All right, all right. I don't want to ruin your fun. But remember, this *is* only a maybe right now and we've seen those go wrong before."

I know he's right. 'Course I do. But right now, I don't care. I say, "Just for maybe's sake, what do you think of putting the mattress straight down on the floor? I'd feel terrible if she rolled out of bed. That floor is hard. Think we could put the bed frame in the garage?"

Marty says, "Okay. I'll move it out there if you want. Hey, did you hear about the fire? The timing of it was crazy. Heck, we were just there."

"Yep. Say, what do you think of decorating the hall powder room to match this bedroom? It would be cute. But it's also the powder room for visitors, so I don't know. I guess it shouldn't be too babyish. All just "maybe" plans at this point, of course."

"Well, we could do something in between. Use the same colors as the bedroom but skip the kiddie stuff? Whatever you want, babe. Somehow, I get the idea that you've thought about this stuff a time or two before."

"Yep. I set that fire, you know."

His smile disappears. "Don't even joke like that."

"Oh, right, toys. And clothes. I'm not sure on the size, though. I hope I get to go shopping for her soon! You can't come. You ain't invited. You're no fun to shop with."

But he continues to glower so I answer him.

"Okay. I set the fire. And no, I ain't joking. Okay?"

"You... How? I was right there."

"When you was boarding up the window. I put crystal balls on all the windowsills, and kindling, too. It was long overdue."

After I got past the shock of seeing the blaze in full color in the newspaper, I felt deep, abiding relief that that Satan's den was gone at last. That, combined with my dinnertime discussion with Betty Lou, had me pretty well giddy, truth be told.

"Christ, Verona." He paces around the room, running his fingers through his hair, like he always does when he's really wound up.

"Language, please." I pick the pad of paper back up and jot down a couple of notes. Shower curtain to use as mattress protector. Curtains, or fabric to make curtains (matching thread).

"You don't understand. I'm the first one the sheriff will come looking for. Did you forget I did time for arson?"

"Why would they come looking for anybody? It was our house, silly." I write, *See Sears* Christmas Wish Book, toddler toy section. Buy toddler toothbrush, baby thermometer.

"Why? Well, for one thing, that house is surrounded by acres of dry scrub land, which could have caught fire and spread. Just because it didn't, doesn't mean there won't be an endangerment charge, for starters." He keeps pacing and raking his fingers through his hair. My joy turns into fear.

He says, "I don't know if we've got a problem or not but I don't like this at all. You should have talked to me before doing something so crazy."

What flashes up in my mind is that any hint of us seeming questionable could make Betty Lou Thomason change her mind about letting us take Amara. Oh, we can't have this. Not now.

"Well, I never thought of that. What should we do?"

He plops down next to me on the bed and we just sit there for a while. Even Talavera is still, watching us through narrowed eyes, from her perch on top of the dresser.

Finally, Marty speaks. "I think our safest bet is to just have the remains of the shack hauled away. That might shut down the possibility of an investigation. There won't be nothing there to investigate. Meanwhile, don't say nothing to nobody. Any authorities come snooping around, tell them your lawyer will get back to them."

"OK, that's a great idea. I'm really sorry for causing all this worry.'

"I know you didn't mean to. Hey, I know a demo guy. I can offer him extra money for a rush job. But see, then that looks suspicious right there, without a reason for the rush job."

I think of children right off, since I seem to be obsessed with children at the moment. "I know. Tell him we want it done right away because some kids was playing in the rubble and we're afraid they'll get hurt. Or we're afraid we could get sued if they get hurt. Something like that."

"Yeah, that'll do. I'll call him now."

VENICE

What I said before was true, that it's delightful to be free of the never-ending demands of a body. That's just common sense. You don't realize what a heavy burden a body is until it's gone. You always had it, so you just don't know.

I didn't get to finish what I was saying earlier, with the aunties whooping it up, from their anticipation of being set free, and from getting to watch my goody-goody sister commit arson right under their noses. I'm here to tell you, after all the years of Verona snubbing them, it was like Mardis Gras up here, when they saw Verona doing something wrong for once.

I was afraid they'd pop the whole goddamn air curtain with their carrying on, and fall down right down on top of my sister in a big ghost auntie cloud. Just imagine the look on her face then!

I have to admit, watching her come into the shack with eyes as big as saucers, holding the cross on her necklace like a goddamn itty-bitty shiv, it really was hysterical.

And I'm as glad as anybody to be freed of that old house. But as for the rest of it, Verona is still my sister and I know she didn't really mean to snub nobody. Ghosts just scare the daylights out of her, always have. She can't help it. The aunties don't understand how that could be, since she's known them all her life, but that's the truth of it.

So, Mama and I stuck up for Verona and that caused the party ruckus to turn into fighting ruckus. Then, as soon as all that bedlam died down, a new ghost auntie showed up, that old woman from the black shantytown, Royal's granny.

I don't know how the hell she got in here in the first place, when she don't live here. It could be the fire opened a space up in the walls before all the walls burned completely down, who knows. Well, old granny Henny tore into me, calling me cracker trash and a white polecat and going on about how we tried to steal another child from her grandson.

The other aunties was still all excited from the crystal ball fire and the fight. The older aunties, especially, are very excitable, not to mention nosey and judgey. So, on top of everything else, Henny started a whole fucking brouhaha about who Jaci's daddy is.

People ain't no better in death than they were in life. It's the same old goddamn person, minus the body and the cares of the world --- and minus anything useful to do with their time.

Anyhow, I just hummed and hummed until they all finally got tired and quit asking nosey questions. I ain't admitting nothing. I'm so glad to be out of there.

Which brings me to the last couple of things I have to say. First, when you die, like I said before, you're free of the body and all its demands. What I didn't get to say is that you're also free of the demands of living people, the responsibilities and obligations --- as much as you want to be. You can check in on people and try to communicate with them, or not. It's completely up to you.

I checked in on Dick, naturally, more than once. Dick did go through with his divorce from Boring Barbara this time. Or rather he just traded her in for a newer model, as the saying goes. I found Dick all cozily paired up with a younger version of Boring Barbara. The girl speaks proper English in a soft voice and she appears to favor cashmere sweaters this winter, along with Chanel perfume and pearls.

Yep, those goddamn pearls hang around her swan-like, college educated neck every goddamn day, just like they do on Beaver Cleaver's mom's neck.

Did I mention that they live in one of those taffy-colored homes overlooking the bay, in the new Sunset Reef subdivision? The exterior of theirs is painted light blue.

Oh, that hurt. It did. And that's not all...

Dick is also being extremely friendly with the night-time maid at his office, and by extremely friendly, I mean screwing her, right on top of his desk after-hours. I saw him shove a pile of papers right onto the floor, in his zeal to get to his extra-curricular activity.

She's a young, pretty single mother. She's sexy, boozy and loud. I know what the new mistress is thinking too. It's pretty obvious. She's thinking that she is more beautiful than Dick's wife (well, Dick's fiancée, so far, but it's the same idea) and wilder in bed and lots more fun. So, naturally, she thinks it's just a matter of time before she takes the fiancée's place. And Dick lets her think it. He tosses a few promises her way now and then, along with a few presents or buckaroos.

But she ain't never, ever gonna get there. Trust me, I get it now. She simply don't have the class he wants in a wife, for the public part of his life and possibly to be the mother of his future children. She don't understand that she is infinitely more disposable than the new-wife-to-be, Dull Deandra.

Dick is that shiny carnival game, where you put in a coin and hold onto the handle (the handle, haha!) and steer the claw with it, in that big clear box, trying to grab the big, valuable prize you crave. You can see that big reward. It's in your grasp.

But all you're ever gonna pull out for yourself is the weird little rubber snake or the cheap plastic yo-yo. But you don't take a hint. You keep putting in more and more of your coins, until they're all gone.

Oh, another thing. Haven't we all always wondered why there's only ghost aunties here and no ghost uncles. The truth is, I still don't know. Nobody does. That's just the way it is. Or rather, the way it *was*.

Anyhow, about getting out of this place… I wouldn't wish that gaggle of ghost aunties on anybody. They ain't bad ex-people, for the most part. It's just that there were so goddamn many of them, for the amount of space available, and no way to get any distance. It was just too much. So, I want to finish by telling y'all to try not to get stuck in a structure, like a house or other building, after you pass through the curtain made of air. It's tempting at first, because you don't realize that you don't need a shelter no more. You're afraid to do without it. But you don't need it. And houses and other buildings tend to get crowded, as we see here, and they're goddamn hard to escape from, once you're in. I don't know why. That's just the way it is.

Instead, to be truly at peace, go it alone, and trust nature. Soar through the open sky, over snow-peaked mountains or a turquoise-colored sea, or at least through the fresh, pine-scented woods. 'Bye now. Be good.

JACI

It's still light out, but I'm in for the night, reading from encyclopedia volume seven (of thirty-three). Amara is snuggled in asleep next to me.

Well, that's what I'm doing until the sound of splashing in the bay yanks my attention away from learning that wild geraniums are perennials and native to the eastern United States.

I grab the bat that I keep by the door. I turn off the boombox, blow out the candles and peek outside, with my plastic children's binoculars.

What is see, is Katie Thomason, coming ashore. Her jeans are soaked from the waist down. An older woman grips Katie's ponytail, as if it's a leash. As if she's just out taking her Katie-dog out for a stroll, across a shallow bay and to my door. It all looks very wrong. I don't like it.

But my heart starts thumping hard when I see who's sloshing along behind Katie and the woman who must be Katie's mama. The woman coming along behind them is Aunt Verona.

There are three loud raps, then, "I know you're in there, Jacinta Josephine Jenson. I heard the music and I saw the light."

The John Jacob Jingleheimer Schmidt song starts up in mind. I creep back to the sleeping bag, ready to cover Amara's mouth to keep her quiet, if I have to.

"Open this door, right now, Missy. Or I will be right back, with the sheriff. You hear me?"

The sheriff. Aunt Verona would probably leave Katie and her mama here to guard the door. I can't see getting myself and Amara into the rowboat, not with them out there. There's no way out.

I open the door. I step aside, to keep from being knocked over as Aunt Verona comes barreling in like a buffalo on black beauties.

She comes in. She snaps, "Get me an ashtray." Setting the tone, that she is in charge. My nerves are going haywire and the way Aunt Verona issues this order, in an imperious tone like "Off with your head," strikes me as hysterical. I hold up my finger like an idiot, open my eyes real wide and say, "SNAFU!"

When I start laughing, Katie starts laughing.

Katie's mama slaps Katie's face.

Immediately, Aunt Verona slaps my face too, as if protocol demands it.

Katie and I stop laughing. But the slap weirdly comforts me. A slap is a punishment an adult gives a child under their care. It says, "I'll straighten you out." It does not say, "I am turning you in for the authorities to straighten out." That's how it registers in my scattered mind, anyway.

Amara wakes, crying. I pick her up. Aunt Verona bustles around, gathering up our clothes. She says, "Your uncle is waiting in the van back on the island. He is not happy with you, either, Miss. Now let's go."

I'm still scared of Aunt Verona when she's mad but not as scared as I used to be, after being on my own. I say, "No thank you. I don't require that."

Aunt Verona steps toward me, hand raised. She says, "Excuse me?" Her eyes look like they're about to pop out of her face, like something in a horror movie at the dollar matinee.

I stand up straighter, trying to shore up my nerve. "I don't have to. For your information, I turned sixteen last week. And I. Am. Married." I hold my left hand out triumphantly, displaying my fake wedding band. But my hand is shaking, which ruins the effect, so I drop it down to my side.

Aunt Verona sets a stack of clothes down and lights a new cigarette. "Get me an ashtray, now!" she barks. I'm not sure why, when she had just stamped her last cigarette out on the floor of my home.

I get my pack of Salems and I light a cigarette too, to remind us both that I'm grown up, too.

Aunt Verona narrows her eyes and stares at my cigarette but she don't say nothing about that. She says, "Who you married to?"

"Chuck Simmons." I glare at Katie, as if just daring her to snitch on me again.

After a long inhale and a long exhale, Aunt Verona says, "Well, we're taking this here baby and that's that."

Aunt Verona pulls the pillowcases off my pillows and fills them with Amara's clothes and toys. She hands one to Mrs. Thomason and one to Katie, then puts her hands out for Amara.

Slowly, tortuously, I hand Amara over.

The door opens and the uninvited visitors climb down the steps, then slosh off through the bay the way they'd come, taking my child with them.

At first, I keep going through the motions of my old routine. I wash, eat and walk the beach, asking people if they want a scrying. I wonder if this is what it's like to be a ghost, just floating around, feeling lost. Being lost.

Once, I woke up at night, thinking I heard Amara say "Mama," but there's only the empty spot next to me where Amara used to sleep.

A few days later, I'm surprised to catch myself feeling okay sometimes. Being a wife or being a mother, or just acting like you're that, ain't easy, that's for sure. But a couple of things have changed now.

I am sixteen, so the truant officer won't be after me anymore. And I don't have a child who I don't have legal rights to no more, so the law won't be after me for that. And Aunt Verona thinks I'm married and therefore a legal adult, so I'm out from under her control now, too.

I'm free. I can go home. I'll take Mama's place as fortune-teller. I fill my laundry basket with belongings, put it in the rowboat and start across the bay. Once ashore, I secure the boat, grab the laundry basket and start walking toward the fortune-telling shack, going home.

I get closer. Things are not right. The shack isn't there. That's impossible. Houses don't just disappear. Where on earth is the shack?

I catch myself looking up at the sky like an idiot, like the shack is the new Chitty Chitty Bang Bang, a house instead of a car, flying through the sky. Or maybe I'm dreaming, and the past few months never happened: Mama's disappearance and death, Chuck, Linda's trailer, Amara, the fishing shack.

Maybe I'll wake up in a minute, in my old bedroom, with Mama nagging me to hurry up so I don't miss the school bus and me being mad about having to get up, having no idea that I am in the last of the good old days.

I walk down the oyster shell driveway. The driveway is still there. But at the end of it, there's only a concrete pad where the shack used to be. It's like the house just flew cleanly away. Maybe I am the new Rip Van Winkle and I'm just now waking up, far into the future.

There are about a dozen large rectangles and squares dug out on our property, at varying

depths. They have blue tarps over them, held up with metal poles. The archeology professor, Mr. Frog or whatever his name was, must have gotten his way at last.

I plunk my laundry basket full of stuff down on the house foundation and sit on top of it.

I light a cigarette, without really being aware of it, until the act is met with silence. No aunties hum. Where are my aunties?

They are family, even though they are annoying. All of my family members, living and dead, are annoying. But that don't mean I want any of them gone. Wait, I stand corrected. Uncle Marty ain't annoying. He's only a family member by marriage, though. So he missed out on the annoying gene.

What is the meaning of this? Am I just meant to be alone, to not have anyone or anything? No family, no friends, no boyfriend, no child, no home. Not even any ancestral ghosts?

A woman's voice cuts into my thoughts. "Little Miss Muffet, sittin' on her tuffet."

Who is that? It don't sound like any of my aunties.

"Haw haw! Look behind your behind, ya silly sausage!"

I spin around. An older black woman walks toward me, carefully stepping around a shoveled-out rectangle.

The woman comes closer, dressed like something out of the eighteen hundreds. She wears a big old white bonnet that looks a century out of place. I wonder if she is a ghost, though I've never seen one in such solid form before. She looks like the Black woman Katie and I saw

that day that seems like a century ago now, except this lady is only old, not ancient.

I light a new cigarette off the old one. The slow inhaling and exhaling steadies my nerves.

The woman, if she's not a ghost, probably wants money. I fish around in my pockets and pull out a crumpled dollar bill. That'll probably get rid of her. I'm in no mood for chit chat right now.

As the woman comes closer, I hold out the dollar bill and a can of corn. I say, "Will this help you out, ma'am?"

She seems to think that's funny. "Haw haw, you ain't gotta pay me to talk to you. You ain't *that* ugly!" She slaps her knee at the hilarity, and falls over.

"Ow! Ahh!" the woman cries, flopping around on the ground.

I sigh, breathing out a cloud of smoke so big Puff the Magic Dragon would be proud of me. The woman must be drunk. I toss my cigarette away and help her up.

"It's goddamn Mama all over again," I mutter, without meaning to. I'm just exhausted, after walking into *The Twilight Zone*, that's all. I put my hand over my mouth. I'm disgusted with myself, after blurting out an insult about my poor, dead Mama.

"Don't you talk about your mama like that!" the woman says, as if reading my mind. "She a white polecat, but she still your mama."

"I'm sorry, ma'am. I didn't mean it. Did Mama know you?" *What's a polecat?*

"Well, she oughter know me! After all, I *am* her onliest chile's mawmaw. Not that the high and mighty cracker princess ever treat me like it."

I nod. The poor soul has lost her marbles.

"Well, come on, then. Let's go home," the woman says.

"Me?"

"Yes, you. What else you gonna do, build a nest?"

I pick up my laundry basket up and follow the old woman home. I don't know why. I just do.

Mercy, that's the woman's name, lives in a one room shanty, on a dirt road that's lined with other shanties like hers. It has a deck cover tacked onto it, above the hard-packed dirt of an outdoor cooking area.

Miss Mercy's small yard is crowded. There's a garden, a shed, an outhouse, and a couple of chickens wandering around. You can see the trash dump, off in the distance. From here, the dump looks real nice, like it's the start of some rolling foothills.

Inside the shanty, a twin-sized iron bed is pushed up against one wall; a small table with two mismatched chairs, against another. Household items and pantry goods fill the place. It's crowded but clean. There's no electric, no running water. After living at the fishing shack for the past few weeks, I feel right at home.

"Now, go on next door and get your daddy to bring over them fish he caught," Miss Mercy says, stepping outside.

She starts pulling carrots out of her garden. "Better shut your mouth, girlie. You'll be catching flies with it, haw-haw. She waves a carrot at the shack to her right. "It's that-away."

I do as I'm told. I may as well humor the old lady. The door in the next shanty over is halfway open, so I knock on the doorframe. Then I move off the doorstep, so nobody can grab me, just in case.

A light-skinned Black man appears in the doorway and stands there, a question on his face. No, his skin is more like golden. And he is gorgeous.

"Need something?" he says, when I just stand there gawking at him like an imbecile. His voice is deep, like Johnny Cash.

"Um, um... Miss Mercy fish. She wants you to fish?" His eyes are golden-colored, too.

He nods and I scurry away, dazed and mortified.

Miss Mercy has the fire going and has put a pot of water on to boil. She's cutting up vegetables. "I'll take that can of corn now," she says. I go inside to get it.

The beautiful man is there when I come back out. Whole, raw fish are piled up on a platter. Miss Mercy snatches the beer bottle out of the beautiful man's hand. She pours the beer that's left in it into her pot.

"See how she do me?" he jokes. My breath catches.

The beautiful man has a small white patch of hair on his head, like mine.

I pick up the can opener and take a lot of time opening the can of corn, grateful to have something to focus on, because the inside of my mind is boinging around like a pinball machine.

Is he really my daddy?

When I finally look up, he's gone. He comes back when the food's just about ready, with a heavy-set dark woman who has a big afro that's dyed orange-ish. She carries a little baby boy, who's even lighter-skinned than the beautiful man. I look closer, trying to figure out how this Black and gold couple made a white baby.

Then I think I might seem too interested for politeness, so I stop looking.

Miss Mercy introduces them to me, as she fixes plates and passes them around. "This my son, Royal. This lil angel here Royal Junior. Oh," she says, like it's an afterthought, "My son wife name Shereesa."

I smile at them and nod. I don't trust myself to talk. But the silence goes on too long. I clear my throat. "Nice to meet y'all. I'm Jaci."

Royal nods. Shereesa crosses her arms. Her lips are pressed together tight. My dyed streak has grown out a little. I feel like they're both looking at it.

The baby starts to fuss.

Miss Mercy says, "Uh-oh. When he smell food, he want some, even though he not big enough to have any yet."

Shereesa says, "He need his bottle." She hands the baby to Royal and goes next door. I move closer to the baby. I put my finger out and he grabs onto it. He might be my brother. *I might have a brother.* I'm still trying to figure out how, though.

Miss Mercy says, talking about me, "It's a crying shame my Mama didn't live long enough to make friends with this lil gal. Let her hold the baby right quick, Royal."

Royal hands the baby over to me. Miss Mercy stops what she's doing and just looks at me and the baby. She is smiling and nodding and I feel like I've done something right, accidentally.

The baby's warm sweet weight reminds me of holding the fat orange cat Aunt Verona used to have, named Morris, after the cat on the Nine Lives cat food commercials. The baby just gazes at my face, all peaceful now. He smells pretty, like Johnson's baby powder. Miss Mercy's right, he is a little angel. I feel like I might love him already. I seem to get along best with people who are barely even people yet.

Shereesa opens the door of the shack next door. Royal takes the baby back. I understand that part of whatever's going on here. After being raised by Mama, with all the boyfriends she had, I know about lovebirds who try to mix in kids they had by other parents. It's most often a mess.

Miss Mercy's family eats without talking. They wolf down what's on their plates, then refill them.

Right after that, they go home. Royal taps me on the shoulder. Shereesa, holding the baby, stands a ways off, watching. Royal says, "Take care of Mama now, you hear?"

I nod to be polite but it seems to me that's a job for him, not me.

Miss Mercy says Royal and his family have to get up early to go visit Shereesa's family in Louisiana. Shereesa's sister is getting married.

I say, "Oh," not knowing what else to say.

"Royal junior ain't hers. He just Royal's."

That seems rude to ask about so I just say, "Oh," again. I help Miss Mercy clean up. Then she starts walking towards her door so I tell her good-bye. "Thanks for supper, ma'am. It was really good."

Miss Mercy turns around. She says, "What's wrong, chile? You mad?"

"No. I'm not mad. Oh, I forgot my stuff. It's inside."

She says, "Git in here and fix you a place to sleep, baby."

"Oh. Okay," I say. It seems kind of weird to sleep here but it's late and I'm tired. She gives me two old fashioned quilts, and tells me to make up a pallet on the floor.

After it's dark inside and quiet and I'm settled in for sleep, I try on some new maybe- information.

My daddy is Black.

I have a brother.

I'm part Black.

I have a crush on my daddy.

I picture the look of horrified glee that would be on Katie's face if I said that last thought to her. I mean, it would be super creepy and weird, except that I only just now met him for the first time, which makes it crazy and hilarious. I picture saying, "SNAFU!" and me and Katie falling all over ourselves laughing.

But the part about being Black, that would be a whole 'nother story. It might be as bad as if people knew I'd lived with ghosts. Maybe even worse, I'm not sure.

Anyhow, a white spot on someone's head wasn't proof of nothing. Not really. It wasn't like a blood test. Heck, even Aunt Verona's orange cat, Morris, had a white spot on his head.

And didn't I used to think one of Mama's boyfriends was my daddy when I was little, just because he brought me candy when he came to see Mama? I even thought the principal at my elementary school was my daddy for a while, for some reason.

I remember now that Miss Mercy came and found me, not the other way around. These people are very poor. It wouldn't be the first time somebody thought the Jenson family was rich just because we own land.

It sounds insane to think anybody would put bleach on their head to try to trick me. On the other hand, lots of things were crazy. Living with ghosts was crazy, for example. Having your house disappear without a trace was crazy, too.

What we've always done about ghosts in my family is just keep our traps shut about it, in front of outsiders. If this Black man is my daddy, I reckon I can just stick with that method of keeping the nosey-roseys out of my business. I decide that's enough thinking for tonight. I am exhausted.

I wake up at the first hint of dawn, thanks to a dang rooster, outside crowing his cockadoodle head off. I pick up my laundry basket full of belongings and slip out the door, then step back in to set half a dozen cans of vegetables and a few dollars just inside the door for Miss Mercy.

I make my way back to the fishing shack on the bay, the sun rising as I walk. I feel like I'm walking through a dream.

January, 1977

JACI

I had decided to just hibernate for the winter as much as possible, or for the coldest part of the year here anyway, since we don't exactly have winters.

So I was out of touch with things like the holidays. I only learned that I'd completely missed Christmas after hearing lots of fireworks off in the distance late one night and realizing it must be New Year's Eve. Not that it made much difference to me, since I don't currently have any family, friends or even acquaintances, alive or dead.

I'm snuggled up in my two sleeping bags, reading encyclopedia volume ten and thinking about an afternoon nap, when I hear a boat motor outside.

I peek out through my children's binoculars, clutching my baseball bat. The boat pulls up. Uncle Marty tends to it, then he helps Aunt Verona step out.

Now what? It don't make sense that Aunt Verona would wait a whole month after Christmas, if she was trying to find me to give me some presents or something like that. So, I figure that whatever she's coming out here for, I probably won't like it.

Through the binoculars, I watch my uncle hand a small child in a life vest over to Aunt Verona. *What on earth.* Had they decided to give Amara back?

I go ahead and open the door before my aunt even gets to it. You ain't stop Hurricane Verona when her mind is set on barging in on you, so you may as well just clear the path and get out of the way.

Aunt Verona sets Amara inside, then finishes climbing up the ladder and coming in herself.

"Mar Mar! Your mama loves you soooo much!" I say, swooping her up and covering her with kisses while she laughs her adorable little Amara laugh.

She looks less babyish, which makes me want to cry. Her hair's up in pigtails high on her head, just like Aunt Verona used to do mine.

Aunt Verona says, "Yes, her mama does love her. That would be me. And so does her big cousin. Which would be you."

Confused, I look outside with my binoculars again, hoping to see Uncle Marty and enlist him on my side, in whatever my aunt is up to now.

But he looks comfortably settled in, in the old lawn chair out there by the boat. He always did try to duck out whenever Aunt Verona got started on one of her rampages. I wish I could duck out, too.

Aunt Verona's words start to sink in then. "You're... what?" I say, still confused. "Whose boat is that?"

"We rented the boat from the marina. I ain't wading through that doggone bay in no January. And did you hear me? Your Uncle Marty and I have legally adopted Amara. Her new name is Amara Jacinta Harris. I went ahead and gave her your name as her middle name, just so you'd know I didn't forget about you."

My manners kick in. "Oh. Thank you, ma'am. I never had anyone named after me before." And here I had thought my aunt didn't even like me no more. "And the adoption. Wow.

I don't know what to say. Um, congratulations." Well. At least I'd be related to Amara in some way now.

"Thank you," my aunt says. They came here to tell me they adopted Amara?

Aunt Verona is sitting on my sleeping bag with me. There's really nowhere else to sit.

Unsure what to do next, I stick with the company manners thing. "Would you like a Coke? I don't have no ice but they're cold because I keep them outside." I start playing pattycake with Amara.

"No thank you. We have come to get you. We ought to be getting the boat back, or they'll charge us for another hour."

I just knew this was more than a social call. I say, cautiously, "Oh. Well, thank you but I don't require that. Thanks for thinking of me, though."

Aunt Verona puffs herself up. She lights a cigarette. I feel like a bomb is about to drop.

"Get me an ashtray," she orders. This again. Aunt Verona's "I'm the boss" signal.

"Here." I hand her an empty Coke can. I light a cigarette, too. Aunt Verona narrows her eyes but she don't say nothing.

I pull Amara up onto my lap, practically like a human shield. I say, "Listen, you can't just *come and get me*. I'm a married woman. I am legally an adult." I think about ordering Aunt Verona to leave, but I don't quite have the nerve.

Aunt Verona tries to stare me down. It makes me nervous. I turn to Amara instead and sing, "The itsy-bitsy spider, went up the waterspout," doing the hand gestures slowly, so Amara can try to copy them.

Aunt Verona smiles. It's her nasty-nice smile. She interrupts my sing-along session. "It might interest you to know that Linda Thomason brought a friend along to the lawyer's office when we met to sign the adoption papers. I believe Linda said she'd brought him along for "moral support," though neither of them looked to me to know much about morals. Anyway, this friend of hers was *very* surprised to learn that we thought he was your husband."

I slump. I drop my face into my hands. *Goddamn Chuck.* I am sunk.

Amara tries to pry my hands off my face. She says, "Peek-a-boo!"

Aunt Verona says, "Now, you can either come with us, or you can let the judge decide whether to send you to a group home or juvenile hall. You won't be a legal adult for two more years, one. And two, for your information, kidnapping *is* against the law."

"She started it," I say.

"Yes, I heard. Linda stole your boyfriend so you stole her child. And then y'all both thought you were just even-steven. And *that* is exactly why we don't need babies raising babies."

She holds her cigarette up like an exclamation mark.

"Yes, ma'am," I say, meekly. I start gathering up my essentials, trying to hold back tears. I came so close to breaking free. I thought I was free. Why can't one dang thing ever go right for me?

"Just get what you need for a couple of days. Uncle Marty will come back for the rest later, honey," Aunt Verona says, softening her stance, now that she'd won.

We turn the boat in at the marina and get into Aunt Verona's old black Cadillac. I sit in back, next to Amara, in her fancy car seat. Her bag full of car toys fills the space between us.

I say, "Does anyone know where my house went?" I bet that's a question not many people have ever said, or heard.

"Oh, that. Do you think we should tell her all about it, Marty? She's old enough." *Old enough?* Aunt Verona never thinks I'm old enough for anything. When I was at her house last summer, she wouldn't even let me go out to the street by myself when the ice cream man came around, and I was fifteen years old.

"All right, but this is family business, so no blabbing. Got it?" Uncle Marty says.

"Yes, sir." I'm just dying to hear this story.

"Okay. Ah, first, you know about your mama, I trust?"

"Yes, sir. I know she passed."

"We're so sorry about that, hon," he says.

"Thanks. So am I." I hurry up and change the subject, not wanting to think about that gaping hole in my chest right now. "And the shack?"

"Well. Bums were breaking in, doing drugs in there and stuff. Your aunt was worried that they might be influencing you, since we didn't know where you were and all. And as you know, she always thought the ghosts were a terrible influence too, and all that jazz. So, she burned the place down."

"Oh yeah, sure she did." I laugh but no one joins in except Amara, who always laughs when anybody else laughs.

He says, "No, really, kid. She did. When I found out about it, I worried that there might be a big police investigation over it, since I did time in jail for arson years ago."

"Oh yeah, sure you did," I say, with less confidence, though I still think he's kidding and I'm getting tired of the jokes. Teasing me about my home being gone is in poor taste.

But he keeps talking, like he's serious. "That whole thing, my arson conviction, had to do with my mother and a drug den that I burned down as a teenager. So now your aunt and I have both burned down a house for a good cause. What a coincidence, huh?"

That swirly thing starts up in my mind again. My uncle, and even more so my aunt, are the only normal grown-ups I know, aside from some teachers, who don't count because they might just act normal at school. They'd have to, to keep their jobs.

Even thinking about my aunt and uncle as the kind of people who go around burning down houses is just too much. I notice Amara's feet, so adorable in her new pink cowgirl boots. I tug the little foot closest to me. I'm rewarded with a giggle. She brings me back to simple, lovely normalcy for a minute.

"So, with both of us, it was a good intent but wrong action kind of thing," Uncle Marty says. "You know, the kind of wrongdoing a well-meaning person could do, with the best intentions?"

Aunt Verona points her Salem wand at me, as if to say, "Nah-nah, remember, you did some wrong things, too."

The point of view they're hinting at ain't fair, though, that we've all done things wrong with good intentions. I am just a teenager. Whereas they are my ideals of how grown-ups should be. We ain't on the same expectation level. But it's too much to try to explain, so I don't.

We're on the bridge now, headed for the mainland. It crosses my mind that I am trapped with psychotic lunatics and should maybe think about jumping into the bay and swimming away, which weirdly cracks me up.

"You think that's funny, Miss?" my aunt says.

"No, ma'am. I just can't picture you two doing anything wrong, that's all. Especially you."

"Ah," she says, nodding like that makes her happy. "So anyway, then your uncle hired a demolition crew to come clear it all away. Because as I learned too late, you can't necessarily just burn down a house without permission, even if you own it."

I just say, "Oh, okay," though I had actually thought of it as my house, not Aunt Verona's, and she don't seem to notice that she left me homeless. Oh well, too late now. I file this latest catastrophe away in my mind with the rest of my catastrophe collection. I seemed to collect catastrophes now like Katie collects matchbooks.

On the mainland, just when I think things can't get any weirder, my uncle pulls into the parking lot of a liquor store. "I'm just gonna pick up some beer. Be right back," he says, and gets out of the car.

"You're letting him get *beer*?"

Aunt Verona says, all serious-like, "Well you know hon, now that our marriage is twenty-one years old, I thought it was time. The legal drinking age is only eighteen, so I took extra precautions."

I laugh. It seems like now that my aunt has a real child to fuss over, my uncle and I have both been promoted. He's been promoted to full adult status and me, to teenage status, at least. I say, "Can I have some beer too?"

She says, "Now you're just talking crazy. But here, have you some animal crackers. Give one to the baby."

I take the bag of little camels, elephants and lions that she holds out.

Aunt Verona says, "Oh, I almost forgot to tell you. You know that archeology professor your mama used to talk about? Well, we gave him permission to dig on the property."

"Yeah, I saw. She used to call him Professor Frog."

Aunt Verona shakes her head. "Your mama was a pistol. They're setting up a permanent exhibit of their finds at the university. The Venice Jenson Memorial Collection. Ain't that nice?"

Mama would have hated it. She didn't want the frog guy digging around there. But that just about summed up

Mama and Aunt Verona, and me too sometimes. We'd all had mostly good intentions with each other, but they had a way of not coming across that way at all. I say, "It's perfect."

Our last stop on the way home was the McDonald's drive-through. After my time at my fishing shack, their house feels like a top-level resort.

There's been some changes, though. A framed portrait from the Olan Mills photography studio hangs on the wall, Aunt Verona and Uncle Marty, with little Amara in between them, her hair done in those dang high-up pigtails. I remember being the treasured little girl of my aunt and uncle myself, part-time at least. They're good parents.

The living room's been taken over with toys, some of which used to be mine: the wooden pull-along beagle on wheels. The big Crissy doll with hair you could pull from inside its head, from short to long and back again. The giant blue ball with a handle that you could bounce on, called a hoppity-hop or something like that. And of course, the toy kitchen with all its adorable little pans and plastic food items.

I remember my aunt baking cookies with me, walking me over to the park to play on the swing set, or just out in the backyard to play in the sprinkler. Yep, my aunt is great with little kids. It's just the big kids and grown-ups she needs help with.

Uncle Marty drank a beer, along with his burger and fries. I thought he looked pretty proud of himself, sitting there with his frosty mug, which cracked me up.

"Oh, I almost forgot," Aunt Verona says, as we finish eating. "Your uncle and I have been thinking about you. We got you something."

I smile weakly. All I want is my freedom. And, as much as things have improved for my aunt and uncle, the truth is, my star has sunk as much as theirs has risen.

I dread starting high school, let alone starting over in a new school district with all new people. It all feels like a giant step backward.

Going back to being bossed for at least two more years, by teachers at school and Aunt Verona here. Suddenly, I can't get enough air, just like on that first night on the beach with

Chuck, after the big fight with Mama. That seems like a lifetime ago now.

Aunt Verona doesn't seem to notice that I'm having a hard time breathing. She returns to the room with a big envelope. "Tell me what you think of this, Miss," she says. In between gulps of air, I open the envelope. The booklet inside is titled, "How to Get Your GED."

It takes a minute to sink in. My breathing starts to normalize. "Wow. I don't even know what to say. I'll definitely read this, tonight." This is pretty dang wonderful!

Aunt Verona says, "Believe it or not, your uncle and I know how it is. We were young once, too."

For the first time, I can see that. My aunt seems to get where I'm coming from now, when she never did before. A GED ain't freedom right this minute, but it's a ton closer than what I was expecting. I jump up and hug her, then I hug Uncle Marty too. I try to hug Amara but she's getting cranky and pushes me away.

I say, "Oh man. I've gotta tell Katie!" and rush to the phone on the kitchen wall. I pick up the receiver. Then, I remember.

Katie's mad at me for taking Amara away. And I'm mad at Katie for snitching on me about it. But, don't that make us even, really? And aren't we sort of family now, anyway? I mean, now we are officially related, through Amara.

I put the phone receiver back in its cradle and start the evening tidying up, while my aunt puts Amara to bed. I'll try to make it right with Katie, but it will have to wait for a different day.

Tales from Miss Ella's Home Jail

The Vase

September 1978

Bobbie Henson ignored Sheriff Earl Schmidt when he asked how she was doing. She was still hopping mad. And when he started pushing her in her wheelchair, she slammed down the wheelchair's brake lever with her free hand. The sheriff stumbled into her.

"Ooh, you *rammed* me. From *behind*. S-E-X offense!" Bobbie shouted down the hospital corridor. She was glad to see him blush.

She didn't even know a woman *could* be arrested for a sex offense, until Sheriff Earl dragged her here the other night. Meanwhile the real perverts were allowed to freely continue ruining her life. Had she, the lawfully wedded wife, *consented* to that? "Davie" and The Problem were probably having a good laugh about all this, right now.

"We don't need none of that, now," the sheriff said, pulling the brake lever back up.

"We didn't need none of that in the first flipping place!"

"Now, Miss Bobbie. I already told you. Based on what I saw and heard, I had to take you into custody. Now it'll be between you and the judge."

"No, what you did was, you saw a stranger with *highly* questionable morals doing lewd and bizarre things outside in broad daylight. Then you believed that stranger when she said *I* made her do it. I wasn't even out there. I wasn't even awake!" She twisted around to glare at him, the best she could, considering that she was handcuffed to the wheelchair.

This is what she got for ever coming back to this hick town. Do one little thing wrong here and it was held against you for the rest of your dang life.

For example, there was that time in kindergarten when she ate Earl Schmidt's paste, the whole jar of it. He'd cried in front of the everyone, because he was a big soft dink, even then. Most likely, that's what this was about, revenge. The paste was delicious, creamy and minty.

Then there was that time in the third grade, when she trapped one of the little Schmidt kids in her parents' garage and made her eat dog food. She forgot which little Schmidt it was, Eva? Emily? There were so many of them.

But she was playing Evil Queen and that was fair treatment in a dungeon. It was only dry dog food anyway. Everybody eats dry dog food sooner or later.

Or was it because of when she used to call another of Earl's little sisters, Ella, "Elephant," on the school bus? He couldn't pin that on her. Half the bus was in on that one.

An old nurse appeared. She stood there with an eyebrow raised, looking like the boss of the world, as only an old nurse can. Bobbie lowered her voice. "Just let me walk, at least."

"Cain't do that, Miss Bobbie. It's against hospital regulations."

"At least gimme a blanket, then. I'm cold." It was humiliating enough to be wheeled out of the hospital by a cop, without gawkers seeing the handcuffs too.

He nodded to the old nurse, who made a passing candy striper go fetch a blanket.

When it arrived, Bobbie tossed it over the arm of the wheelchair, covering her handcuffed wrist.

"Don't you want the blanket around your shoulders?"

"No, Earl, you big dink."

She wasn't sure if he coughed or laughed, behind her.

They proceeded to the elevator, then outside to his patrol car. Now that her three-day stay for "psychiatric observation" was over, she would be transported to jail.

As they started over the bridge across the bay, she said, from the back seat, "So, you're taking me to your cuckoo-banana sister's home jail?"

"Aw, I thought you two was friends. But to answer your question, yes ma'am. That's where we take the island ladies now. We ran out of room at the main jail, what with so many more people moving to the island and everything."

Watching the bay from the back of the patrol car distracted Bobbie from her misery. The water sparkled in the sunlight, like diamonds on coffee. No doubt it was the last pretty scenery she'd see for a while.

The rest of the ride was quiet, aside from occasional voices on the staticky cop radio.

She was mildly interested in the new women's jail when they pulled up in front. It was definitely strange enough to take notice of. The jail was actually the house the Schmidt kids had grown up in. Now it had burglar bars on the windows, but you couldn't tell that the bars were meant to keep people in rather than out. From the outside, you couldn't tell the place was a jail at all.

Bobbie would have been highly alarmed to be taken to this old rambling ranch house instead of a real jail, if she hadn't known Earl and Ella all her life (and known what goody-goody gumdrops they both were, too).

Inside, Ella Schmidt, *Warden* Schmidt, waited with a Polaroid camera. "Say cheese," she said. After snapping Bobbie's photo, Ella said, "Okay darlin', now come with me."

The home's inside walls had been removed, as had the entire kitchen. There was a little office alcove, with a desk and shelves, near the front door. Six large cages hung from the ceiling, three on each side of the huge room. And two outdoor picnic tables had been placed end-to-end between the two rows of cages. The far wall had a back door and a bathroom door, and a TV mounted on a high shelf.

The scene was straight out of a psycho horror flick, but Bobbie already knew that from Isla Ajaja gossip.

Someone had painted a book title on the wall above the TV, in flowing letters. *I Know Why the Caged Bird Sings by Maya Angelou.* Bobbie had heard of that book but she hadn't read it.

Two of the cages on the left side were occupied, with an empty cage between them. The two women in the occupied cages started rocking their enclosures, repeatedly crashing them into the empty cage in the middle.

"Girls, that'll do," Ella said.

They stopped, apparently more interested in the newcomer than in keeping up the ruckus.

"What you in for?" the hefty Black woman in the closest cage said. She looked vaguely familiar to Bobbie.

"Nothin'," Bobbie said.

"Nothin'," mimicked the skinny White girl in the other cage.

Bobbie shoved the White girl's cage, hard enough to make it crash into the empty middle cage, then ricochet off the wall. "What did you say?" Bobbie said with feigned innocence. She knew from her school days that you had to let the other girls know they couldn't push you around.

"I said that's enough!" Ella snapped. She directed Bobbie into the middle cage, then shut and locked the door behind her. Ella then proceeded to drape large white bed sheets over all three occupied cages.

Bobbie lay down on the mat in her cage. Wasn't covering up the cage what you did with a bird, to calm it down? Oh, the caged bird saying on the wall, the big bird cages. Now it fell into place. Leave it to Ella Schmidt to give a jail a theme, like it was a children's birthday party. And the theme was .. jail birds! Well. At least the bird theme made some kind of sense now, though it was still stupid.

Her mood brightened. This might even be fun, in a kooky way. It was definitely better than being locked up in a real jail, a possibility she'd been sick with fear about in the hospital.

A Few Weeks Earlier

Roberta "Bobbie" Henson painted all day again, in rhythm to the songs on the radio. It was pleasant, like meditating. You just had to turn on some music and get into the right mindset for it.

But who'd have thought a two-bedroom duplex would have so much wall (and ceiling) area to cover. And who'd have thought Dave would dump the whole fixer-upper project on her. He was the one who'd insisted on buying the rundown duplex building in the first place.

"Live in one side and rent out the other," he kept saying. "It'll help us get a start." She was 39 and he was 37, and this was a second marriage for them both. She thought they ought to have been far beyond "getting a start" by now.

They'd barely finished unpacking when Dave took on more hours at work. A lot more hours. which he volunteered for without consulting her. It made her mad, a slow but deep burn.

He knew she'd wanted to get a job herself, after the miscarriage. But between them only having one car and the big fixer-upper project now, it seemed more sensible for her to do this instead, for now. Especially since he'd practically demanded it.

Staying home was boring and lonely, especially with him working late nearly every night now.

"This wasn't the deal, you know," she'd remind him, then get mad all over again when he had the nerve to reply, "I'm helping us get a start." It was like he somehow didn't count the money she could earn, and had earned in the past, as helping with this "start in life." Granted, she'd always only made the minimum wage, but she fumed at his attitude that her contributions wouldn't count at all.

After cleaning up for the day, Bobbie grabbed the jug of Gallo Burgundy from the fridge and drank straight from the bottle, sitting cross-legged on the floor. Boxes and bags were piled high in the middle of the room: new light fixtures, wall switches, bathroom vanity tops and drapery rods.

Hopefully, she'd finish the painting this week, before the carpet installers came. She watched out the window for Dave's car.

She'd had her heart set on the peach-colored house in the new Sunset Reef subdivision. It was one of the smaller models and not bayfront, but the whole development had a swanky resort feel about it. There was a big showy fountain at the entrance, and palm, orange, and banana trees everywhere. A pool and clubhouse overlooked the boat slips on the bay. Living there would be like a permanent high-class vacation.

Oh well. She had to admit transforming these crazy hippie wall colors to a fresh, calm shade throughout was satisfying. (color: Victorian lace). Maybe they'd be able to move to Sunset Reef in a few years. Surely, they'd have a kid by then, maybe even two.

Oh, there was Dave's Mustang, finally. She put the wine back in the fridge and headed to their home next door. She debated whether to greet him with a kiss or the angry words that lived on the tip of her tongue, ever since he'd started making all their decisions by himself.

After giving the unit a final vacuuming, Bobbie indulged herself with a walk-through, savoring each freshly remodeled room. Then she settled in on the new carpet (color: golden sand) with her notebook and started working on the rental ad. She consulted *The Daily News* rental section for ideas on how to word it:

2/2 duplex apartment with carport. Stove/oven and refrigerator included. Newly remodeled. One year lease. References required. No pets. $200 per month, plus $200 security deposit. Available immediately.

She'd wanted them to move over to this freshly redone side of the duplex, but Dave said no. A knock at the door interrupted her thoughts.

She peered through the peephole. A lanky, dark-haired girl stood on the porch. Bobbie opened the door.

Before Bobbie could say anything, the girl said, "We need to talk."

The girl's confidential tone grated on Bobbie's nerves. Who would fall for that old sales tactic. "What do you need?" she said, shutting the door partway. She didn't feel like hearing about Jesus, encyclopedia sets, or whatever the kid was pushing.

The girl said, "It's about Davie."

"Who's Davie?"

"Um, can I just come in for a sec? I, like, really want to get this over with."

Bobbie felt the walls waver a bit. Suddenly, she knew what was coming. She just knew. Just like with her ex. She led the girl to a spot on the carpet and sat down.

The girl remained standing. "So, I'm Debbie. And Davie and I are, like, in love. With each other."

The dreadful words hung in the air, surreal.

"We didn't mean for it to happen. It just, like, did. And now, we need to be together. Like, me and Davie, I mean."

Bobbie stared at the girl.

"Davie loves me. Not you," the girl said proudly, as if expecting a first-place ribbon at the county fair.

Bobbie didn't like this problem named Debbie standing over her. Bobbie was on the floor at The Problem's feet, as if the girl was Bobbie's superior.

Bobbie coiled back, then sprung, now a wild, wounded beast. She snatched up a handful of the girl's hair at the scalp and dragged her down the hall.

"Ah! Like, lemme go!" the girl said, followed by some unusual squawks.

Bobbie was too busy to answer, flipping up the toilet seat, then trying to push the girl's head into the bowl. It proved harder than expected. She just wouldn't bend. "I just cleaned it!" Bobbie yelled, as if that should make the girl more cooperative.

116

"Ow! You're, like, crazy!"

"You're crazy! And sleazy. And a... toilet head."
Bobbie shoved the girl's head and said her words in a rhythm.
She finally settled for dipping the ends of the girl's hair into
the toilet water.

All at once, Bobbie felt drained. "Just leave," she said.
She was too weary to even enjoy seeing the girl's smug
expression turned to one of terror.

The girl fled.

It was just like Dave, when she thought about it, to hide
behind a teenage girl, or whatever ridiculously young age The
Problem was.

Bobbie didn't know if Dave was aware of Debbie's
visit or not. He didn't say a word about it. Neither did Bobbie.

When she'd caught her ex-husband cheating, Bobbie
punched him in the face, gave him a black eye. It was among
her most treasured memories. Revenge was the best therapy.

But this time was different. She was older now. Her
last chance to have a family of her own was slipping away.
She thought she'd do just about anything to keep Dave, even
though she kind of hated him now.

Davie and Debbie. David and Debra. Dave and Deb.
They were the kind of go-together names she and Dave might
have picked for their future children. She needed to win Dave
back ASAP.

First, she'd run The Problem off. Then she'd get even
with Dave.

Bobbie bleached her hair. She started doing her
makeup each morning, even on the days she didn't plan to
leave the house. She put on cute clothes and even bought a
couple of new outfits. She counted calories and exercised
along with Jack Lalanne on TV. She laid out in the sun to
maintain a sun-kissed complexion.

She stopped complaining and she had a nice dinner
waiting every night. She initiated lovemaking, which Dave
sometimes responded to and sometimes did not. She stayed in

bed afterwards, with a pillow under her hips, to help facilitate pregnancy.

One Saturday, she told Dave she was going to the grocery store. He requested pork rinds and braunschweiger as she kissed him good-bye. She wrote his requests on her shopping list without even making a face, though both items were nasty and so was he.

Dave moved next door while she was gone, into the unit she'd just finished remodeling.

Bobbie was still putting the groceries away, robotically, stunned, when an old blue Chevy pulled up. The Problem got out and opened the trunk.

The Problem trudged toward the unit next door, lugging two large, full trash bags.

Something about the timidity of her movements, in combination with her unbelievable audacity, activated Bobbie's fury again. She sprang into action.

"Whoa, ah, stop it!" The Problem cried, dropping her bags as Bobbie rammed into her.

Bobbie bounced The Problem's head off the driveway a couple of times. She snatched up the girl's trash bags and shoved them down the storm sewer at the street. She had to rip the bags open so everything would fit through the sewer opening.

She clapped her hands together on the way back to her unit, dusting them off, like *that's that*. The new drapes she'd hung in the front window next door (color: white cliffs of Dover) moved, ever so slightly.

So, "Davie" was watching. How much could he care about The Problem, really, if he'd just stood there watching Bobbie kick The Problem's hind end up and down the street?

Ten minutes later, an officer of the law knocked on Bobbie's door.

"Good afternoon. Got a call about you assaulting your husband's, er, girlfriend? And you threw her belongings into the storm sewer?" Sheriff Earl Schmidt was acting all official, like they hadn't known each other all their lives.

"No sir. They lie. They try to make people think that it's me doing wrong instead of them." She lowered her gaze, innocently.

He may have been fighting back a smile, she couldn't tell for sure. "Well, alrighty then, ma'am. Like I told them, we don't typically get involved in domestic disputes. Just try to keep yourself *to yourself* from now on, hear? We don't need no trouble around here."

"But I didn't ---"

"Have a nice day, ma'am." He tipped his hat and walked away.

"Davie" arrived home promptly at 5:30 every weeknight now, at his new residence, the whorehouse next door.

Bobbie made her self-improvement schedule even stricter. She'd become irresistible.

Then Dave would come home.

She picked a slightly different shade of white for this side of the duplex (color: cream puff). The names of the paint shades she'd chosen for the unit next door made her slightly ill now.

Bobbie's daily schedule included: diet, exercise, tanning, getting dolled up daily and fixing up this side of the duplex. She also took up oil painting. She painted along with Bob Ross on the TV in the afternoons. His voice soothed her, as she learned to paint trees and skies and to not worry about mistakes, or "happy accidents," as he called them. Developing a talent would make her more interesting to Dave.

Dave suffered from a midlife crisis, obviously. She'd be ready when his bout of insanity and pedophilia ended. He'd come home to a remodeled home and a remodeled wife.

She pictured the two of them starting over with a second honeymoon. She'd ordered Hawaiian brochures from the travel agency.

Bobbie's self-improvement schedule kept her busy during the day. At night, she drank Gallo Burgundy from the jug and thought about how to get rid of The Problem.

One night, she got the extra key to Dave's car --- her and Dave's car--- from her kitchen junk drawer, crept outside and opened the car door. She flung an enormous pair of women's briefs into the back seat. She'd come across them at the dime store a few days earlier, while picking out sexy lingerie to wear when Dave came home.

Safely back in her unit now, she burst into a howling laughing fit that turned into sobbing somewhere along the way.

Another night, she tossed a lipstick into his car.

Then an earring.

Something finally paid off, judging by the muffled arguing and crying she heard now.

But she couldn't make out the words, even with the old trick of pressing a cup against the wall and pressing her ear to the bottom of the cup.

The ladder was propped against the wall where she'd been painting in the bedroom. And the attic access was on the ceiling right above it. Maybe she'd be able to hear better from the attic.

The attic access panel in the ceiling pushed aside easily. Up she climbed, her and her flashlight.

To her surprise, the attic was wide open. No wall separated the two units up here. She tiptoed over to the next-door unit, and carefully slid the attic access panel there aside a crack.

She looked down, into the master bedroom next door.

Finally, Bobbie's unit was repainted. The place looked light and airy. It was a job well done. She opened a couple of windows to clear out the paint fumes.

She heard something out back, possibly a dog or raccoon. She looked out… to see The Problem rooting around in the yard. A patch of grass over there was dug up. *The Problem had dared to plant something.*

A couple of evenings later, Dave pulled in next door at 5:30 sharp. His new promptness continued to feel like a slap every night. Apparently, the whole extra hours at work bit had been a lie. And she'd fallen for it. After her previous marriage, she should have recognized the signs.

The Problem came running out of their unit and hopped into Dave's car. Just like she undoubtedly had in high school, whenever any boy at all pulled up in front of her parents' house and honked, Bobbie thought. The two of them drove off in Dave's car. *Bobbie and Dave's car.*

Bobbie moseyed over to their backyard. Marigolds and zinnias. She yanked up most of the plants, ripped them apart and tossed them back onto the dirt. It was hilarious.

Now to have a looky-loo around inside. She entered her own unit, climbed up into the attic, and dropped down into the other side. She hadn't been able to find the spare key.

It was very neat inside, no mess anywhere. The Problem was clearly trying to top her. *Oh look, Davie. Whatever your wife wasn't, I most certainly am. I'm, like, so much neater, thinner, younger, cuter. And nicer!*

The Problem was like that old song, "How Much is That Doggie in the Window." The Problem was the doggie, hopping up and down in the window, wagging her tail, desperately doing absolutely anything to be the one chosen. *Pathetic.*

Bobbie got a good look at the new furniture she'd seen carried in from various delivery trucks. A king-sized waterbed took up most of the bedroom. The ruffly pink bedspread didn't go with it at all. It was like Little Bo Peep in a hippie commune. No taste at all.

She tossed a prissy pink pillow onto the floor. She grabbed the dirty laundry basket from the closet and scattered its contents on the floor, too. Then she picked up a pair of tiny black bikini underwear and stretched them over the lampshade, just to be funny.

The new living room set made her furious, an ugly, pink-flowered sofa and loveseat. A coffee and end table set with weird gingerbread accents tacked onto their sides.

Does Minnie Pearl live here? Stupid!

The furniture was, no doubt, bought with her and Dave's savings, their "start in life." Dave had been upset last year when Bobbie splurged on a new shower curtain and a pair of bedside lamps from K-Mart.

Back home, Bobbie laughed herself into tears again. This is what Dave had reduced her to. She could practically hear The Problem's whiney voice now, as she'd heard from the attic before: She's crazy! Like, why won't the fat old bitch leave us alone!

Like, Bobbie planned to give The Problem something to whine about.

After running her fingers through her hair to straighten it after sleep, a quick breakfast of six Twinkies and a few gulps of wine, Bobbie was ready.

She climbed up into the attic, shoved the next-door attic access panel out of the way and swung down into the bedroom. The Problem was just coming out of the bathroom, wrapped in a pink towel. All the pink in this place was sickening but of course it was just right for Debbie, AKA trailer park Barbie.

"What the fuck are you doing here?" The Problem dared to say, as she scuttled back into the bathroom.

Bobbie didn't care for The Problem's language. She went to the kitchen and brought back a chair to sit on, after flinging its tacky pink-striped seat cushion across the room. She settled in, keeping a hold on the bathroom doorknob. The girl could just stay in the bathroom for a while.

She belonged in the bathroom.

Eventually, The Problem dared to try and come out. She tried to turn the doorknob once. And again, then a half dozen times in quick succession. She said, "Ah! Let me out! You're, like, crazy!"

Bobbie didn't feel like conversing with The Problem so she simply held onto the doorknob.

The Problem began to weep. A glow of mean happiness radiated out from Bobbie's heart and spread through her chest.

The Problem said, "Could you go home now, Miss Bobbie? Please?"

Well, that was a better attitude, at least. Bobbie said, "Uh, I *am* home. This property has *my* name on it, so I'll come in whenever I feel like it. I can make you leave any time too, if

I feel like it, whether Dave likes it or not. And don't you forget it."

She had no idea if any of that was true or not.

After a while, Bobbie got tired of holding the doorknob. Her arm hurt. She opened the door and grabbed The Problem by its hair. "I command you to get dressed and get me a Pepsi right this minute, peon. With ice, dagnabbit!" she said, stamping her foot, slipping back into the Evil Queen role, a game she'd enjoyed as a child.

Bobbie removed the handpiece from the phone on the nightstand. She removed the handpiece from the kitchen wall phone, too. I would be just like the little skunk to call the cops on Bobbie for a minor "wrong" done to herself, after monstrously destroying Bobbie's whole life behind Bobbie's back.

Bobbie settled in on the ugly, pink-flowered sofa, with both phone receivers safely beside her.

The Problem came out wearing jean cut-offs and a t-shirt with a big penile looking mushroom applique on it.

"Get in there and change that highly indecent shirt, this very instant, you trash heap. I command you to!"

"Why? Whyyy?" The Problem whined, as if under the impression that Queen Bobbie would be swayed by a wheedling baby voice.

"Because I said so, subhuman!" Queen Bobbie thundered, slapping her palms down hard on the ugly coffee table.

The Problem scuttled down the hall. Queen Bobbie howled with laughter. It was a shame they wouldn't have any dog food here. Maybe she'd make The Problem eat some toilet paper or something.

The Problem returned, wearing a baggy red t-shirt. She went to the kitchen and brought back two sodas on ice. She handed one to Queen Bobbie, who thought this was too easy. The Problem was probably up to something. Probably trying to poison her.

Queen Bobbie snatched The Problem's soda from the coffee table and put her own soda in its place. "Drink that," she said. "Also, you sit on the floor."

Queen Bobbie watched as The Problem moved to the floor and took a couple of big sips of soda. Queen Bobbie waited with interest, to see if The Problem died or anything.

After enough time had passed that it seemed likely The Problem would live, Queen Bobbie said, "I command you to turn on the TV, stupid. Put on *The Hollywood Squares*."

Wait. Who said The Problem could have a Pepsi? Infuriated, Queen Bobbie snatched up The Problem's soda and poured it into the potted palm in the corner, tittering when the pot overflowed and seeped dirty soda water onto the carpet. She sat back to enjoy her soda, the TV

game show, and her position as queen.

After *The Hollywood Squares* ended, The Problem whined, "May I use the restroom?"

"Silence! I shall now leave, as I'm quite bored by you." She dumped the ice left in her glass out on the carpet, snapped her fingers and said, "I command you to clean that up, this very second, peasant!" She left by the front door, feeling quite puffy and luxuriant.

Bobbie was stationed at the next door's attic access at 5:30 pm sharp, with the attic access lid cracked just a tad, so she could hear better.

She lay there listening for hours, until she was sure they were asleep. Her name never came up. She didn't know what to think about that.

Bobbie tossed and turned in bed, enraged. How dare that nasty, mealy mouthed little swamp creature think she could sneak in and steal Bobbie's life!

The birds outside started chirping just before dawn. Bobbie gave up on sleep and headed for the jug of wine in the fridge.

A couple of hours later, she heard Dave's car start up outside. She waited a while longer, taking a few more gulps of wine.

The Problem's eyes widened when Bobbie's head popped down from the ceiling. The Problem dared to say, "Oh, no."

"Oh, yes. Peep-o!" Queen Bobbie swung down into the bedroom. She retrieved a chair from the kitchen, stood on it and pulled the jug of wine down after her.

"I order you to tell me about the flowers you had the nerve to plant in my yard without permission." The Problem backed up as Queen Bobbie approached, until pressed against the wall. "I, like, love flowers."

"That's it? That's all you got? Get thee in the outhouse!"

The Problem scurried into the bathroom and shut the door. She arrogantly locked it without permission.

Queen Bobbie wedged the kitchen chair under the doorknob so The Problem couldn't get out.

Bobbie stumbled out the back door and pulled up a few flowers from the patch in the yard. She sat down in the grass for a while and made herself a flower crown.

Bobbie remembered going back into the house with a bunch of pulled up flower plants and stopping to take a couple more swigs of wine.

What happened after that was murky.

Bobbie awoke on the ugly sofa, with Sheriff Schmidt cuffing her wrists behind her back.

"You're under arrest," he said.

"Huh? What for?"

Sexual assault," he said. "You have the right to remain silent..."

The paste was what started the conversation. Ella put a big jar of LePage white school paste on the picnic table, which reminded Bobbie of eating Earl Schmidt's paste in kindergarten.

One thing led to another, and the two other girls coaxed her into telling her story. She found herself telling it.

"So, the sheriff happened to drive by, and apparently, the girl was naked and in the tripod position, right there on the front porch, in broad daylight. With flowers sticking out of you-know-where," Bobbie said to Shaneisha and May.

They were doing one of Ella's silly self-improvement activities. "Anyone seen the scissors?" Bobbie said.

"Are you fucking serious--?" May started, horrified. Shaneisha pinched her leg under the table, not wanting Bobbie to stop talking.

"Here you go," Shaneisha said, pushing the children's scissors across the table. "Naked and in the tripod position, really?"

"I know, can you even believe it? She told the sheriff that I made her do it. I mean, I'm not even awake, and Sheriff Earl has known me all his life, mind y'all. Yet he takes the word of some teenage problem child over mine, especially one who thinks she's a flipping vase?"

Shaneisha and May exchanged a look.

Bobbie pressed her lips together. These two could certainly be judgy for a couple of criminals. "Anyhow, even if I did *very drunkenly* say something like that, which I didn't, so what? I mean, what if I got drunk and told you to go streaking, steal a car, then jump off a flipping bridge. If you did it, whose fault would that be?"

In the long silence that followed, Bobbie made a mental note to keep her business to herself from now on. Who cared about these trashy girls anyway, with their multiple arrests.

They were beneath her.

Bobbie turned back to the activity, a piece of paper that said "Relationship Pizza" at the top and had a big circle in the center, which was supposed to be a pizza crust. Another page was titled "The Ingredients of a Good Relationship." It had the outlines of pizza ingredients. You were supposed to color those in, cut them out, and paste them onto your "pizza."

Tomato sauce = Friendship
Cheese = Respect
Mushrooms = Kindness
Pepperoni = Fairness
Onion = Honesty

Shaneisha, looking down at her project, said, "Guess my relationship wasn't nothing but a plain crust."

"Mine too," Bobbie said, eager to move on to a different topic.

May said, "Not mine. Mine has double everything."

"Oh hush. You're just a pup," Shaneisha said.

"Yeah. Just wait, kid," Bobbie said. She and Shaneisha were the ones to exchange a look now. Bobbie liked this much better.

"Who wants supper?" Warden Ella said, coming through the back door with a big tray of food.

Shaneisha and May made bird sounds. Shaneisha said "peep, peep," and May said "quack, quack." Bobbie didn't say anything because it was stupid.

Bobbie looked across the room at the new girl and they both shook their heads. The new girl had just been brought in and stuck in a cage about an hour ago. Bobbie didn't remember her name.

Ella opened Bobbie's cage and handed her a plate: barbecued chicken, green beans, potato salad, apple sauce and a buttered roll. Ella said, "Here's you some ice water. It's all I got to drink right now."

It looked wonderful. But Bobbie didn't feel like thanking her captor, so she just started eating.

Ella handed the same meals and drinks to Shaneisha and the new girl.

Then Ella opened May's cage and handed her a plate -- - with nothing on it at all. "And here's yours, May," she said. "Quack!" May shrieked, right in Ella's face. Bobbie and the new girl, startled, cracked up laughing. Maybe the new girl was going to be all right.

May leaned back against her cage bars, examining the empty plate as if trying to make sense of it.

Ella pulled her desk chair over so she could face all of them at once. "Now, what did y'all notice about tonight's suppers?"

Shaneisha said, "We can't come out and eat at the table."

"That's right," Ella said. "There's been a lot of rudeness today, so that's what y'all get. In other words, that's the *consequence* for y'all's *actions*. What else do you notice?"

Good lord. Ella thought she was running the *Romper Room* children's show.

The new girl pointed at May and said, "That girl didn't get any food."

"Right! And ain't that life? We don't all get the same on our plate, do we?" Ella said, pleased.

May banged her empty plate against the cage bars in protest.

Ella said, "So, what do we do when life don't give us our fair share? Feel sorry for ourself? Throw a tantrum and get in trouble? Does that fix the problem?"

Shaneisha, nibbling on a drumstick, said, "Nope, it don't."

"Suck up," May muttered, then returned to slapping her plate against the bars.

Ella ignored May. She said, "What should we do, when we don't get what we need?"

"Try to get it?" Shaneisha said. May glared at her.

"Good!" Ella clapped. "And what are some ways we could try?"

"Ask for it?" the new girl said.

"Good! That's definitely one way. Of course, no one way works for *every* situation in life. But ya gotta stop and think, "What is the *best* way to get what I want?" The best way would be calm, logical and *legal*. Right, girls?"

"Yep," said Shaneisha. Her going along with Ella inspired May to rock her cage into Bobbie's, so Bobbie's cage would bang into Shaneisha's.

"That's enough," Ella said, clapping her hands together.

Ella and the girls, besides May, ate. May lay on her mat, facing the wall.

Bobbie felt sorry for May. May was sensitive to slights and she hadn't even done anything wrong, for once. Bobbie tried to toss a chicken drumstick into May's cage. But it bounced off the bars and plopped wetly to the floor.

"Fuck you," May muttered.

"Uh, I was *trying* to give you something to eat. You're *welcome*," Bobbie said.

New Girl said, "Miss Ella, can May have some food too?"

"Yes!" Ella squealed, practically out of her mind with joy. "Now, y'all see? Ain't that better than hitting the empty plate on the bars? And ain't that better than throwing food that ends up on the floor? See, ya just gotta slow down and ya gotta think. Think *before* you act."

Ella went through the back door and came back with May's supper. "And what else did we learn?" She said, after handing May her plate. "Well, I'll tell you what. That there are plenty of people around who *want* to help us!"

May ate, her face so pouty that the other three girls couldn't help but share a laugh about it.

A few days later, Bobbie's court-appointed lawyer stopped by to tell her that the charges against her had been dropped. There wasn't enough evidence to proceed because The Problem could not be located.

Twenty minutes later, a dazed Bobbie stood outside waiting for a cab, in the clothes she'd arrived in several weeks earlier. She held a big folder full of her completed assignments from Ella. Ella would have been a great kindergarten teacher.

When Bobbie entered her duplex, she had the sensation that she was walking into the life of someone else. She looked around at the fresh paint throughout, the ceramic owl cookie jar on the counter, the light coming in through the windows. It was a nice place. She felt extremely fortunate.

Then she saw the big wine jug, on its side on the floor, and the pool of dried red wine on the carpet. She shuddered. That was the behavior of a real demento, someone she wouldn't want to know, let alone be.

She cleaned up the wine stain the best she could, then got the rug from the master bathroom floor and placed it on top of the wine stain. She didn't want to see any reminders of that terrible day or the terrible weeks leading up to it.

She got the bucket and bleach from the utility closet and went to work cleaning out the refrigerator.

Once that nastiness was dealt with, she decided to celebrate her freedom by ordering a pizza.

While she waited for her pizza to arrive, she turned on the TV, *her* TV. *Gunsmoke* wasn't her favorite, but it was nice to be able to turn it on without asking permission.

The doorbell rang. She grabbed her wallet and opened the door, expecting the pizza delivery boy.

It was Dave.

He smelled like men's cologne, as he had when they were dating. He held up a new jug of Gallo Burgundy. "Hey, sweetie. Can I come in?"

She moved aside and let him in, out of habit or surprise. The pizza guy pulled up before she got the door shut. *Damn. Now she'd have to share.* She'd wanted to save half the pizza for tomorrow's lunch.

Dave pulled two wine glasses out of the cabinet. She didn't like him getting into her cabinet like he still had that right. "Oh, I don't want any," she said. She pushed past him to get two plates and some napkins.

"No wine?" He seemed shocked, which annoyed her.

"No thanks." She didn't plan to drink wine again for quite a while, if ever.

He settled in next to her on the sofa. She got up, pretending to use the bathroom. When she returned, she sat on the loveseat instead.

He said, "Debbie and I are over. Man, that was insane. I guess it was just a midlife crisis. I got tired of her pretty soon, though. There's just not much to her. It's like she's not *finished* or something."

"Well, she is young enough to be our child. So, there's that."

"Yeah. I've learned my lesson. This whole thing has just made me realize for sure that my place is with you."

Bobbie chewed her pizza. Ham, onion and pineapple, her favorite. The pineapple reminded her of the Hawaiian second honeymoon she used to want. Now she was satisfied

with being right here, in her own place, on her own sofa,
watching her own TV and eating whatever she wanted.

Her gut reaction to Dave was nothingness, with a touch
of ick. Like he was just some guy she'd gone on a date with
and knew right away that there'd be no second date. She
thought of Ella's little coloring lesson, with the relationship
pizza.

"Dave, I think the time for you and me is in the past."

"What? You mean... You're just going to throw it all
away?" His eyes filled with tears. "Let's start over. What
about a baby?"

"To tell you the truth, Dave, I'd rather if you left."

"Fine, bitch." He grabbed another slice of pizza, then
stormed out, slamming the door.

She locked the deadbolt after him. *What a dink.*

The phone rang. And rang. She took the receiver off
the hook. She put the leftover pizza on a plate, covered it with
plastic wrap, and placed it in her sparkling clean refrigerator.

Dave beat on her door. He rang her doorbell over and
over again. Bobbie went to her bedroom and searched for
something to read. She was pleased to find *The Thorn Birds*,
which she'd started on a while back, then forgot all about.

She was cozy in her own bed, in her jammies with the
smiley faces all over them, instead of a jail jumpsuit. She read
for a while by the light of her bedside lamp. With pillows
plumped up all around her, she felt very, very fortunate. The
solidness of the bed felt strange, though. It didn't sway like the
jail cage.

She wondered what the girls at Ella's home jail were
doing right now. Maybe she'd go visit them. But she caught
herself right away and shook her head at that stupid thought.

After a while, Bobbie turned off the lamp. Tomorrow,
she'd walk to the corner store to pick up some groceries and a
copy of *The Daily News.* She'd look at the Help Wanted
section.

She'd pick out a divorce attorney from the *Yellow
Pages.*

She was thinking maybe sometime after she got it all
together, she might even call the County Child Welfare and
see what the prospects were for a single woman such as

herself to εdopt a child. After all, she had only been *suspected* of a crime, not convicted.

She knew it would take time. But taking one step at a time to get a start in a new, improved life suddenly seemed quite do-able. Nearly as simple as one of Ella's little lessons.

The Family Dance

April, 1983

"Rise and shine!" Miss Nancy practically shouted, in her fried nasal voice.

"Wow. That dream again. Seemed like it was real," Sugar said, rubbing her eyes, hiding her annoyance at being awoken so abruptly.

Miss Nancy set two cups of coffee on the nightstand, then plopped herself down on the end of the bed, uninvited.

"Being overheated causes vivid dreams. Like fever dreams, you know."

It *was* hot up here in the old servants' quarters. Even now, first thing in the morning.

Sugar's dreams were about a real-life girl named Marvella, who was featured in a book about the old poorhouse that used to be on the mainland, on the other side of the bay.

Miss Nancy took Sugar to the little island library every week. Sugar hadn't looked forward to picking out a local history book, but it was one of the requirements on her reading list.

She'd grabbed the book about the poorhouse randomly, expecting to be bored. Instead, she found Marvella in its pages.

Marvella had been rented out as live-in domestic help, just like Sugar was. But Marvella was born a century ago and was rented out from the poorhouse. Sugar, herself, was rented out from Miss Ella's home jail. It wasn't hard to see the connections a dreaming mind might make.

Sugar carefully tore the picture of young Marvella out of the book and put it in her nightstand drawer. She took it out and gazed at it often, secretly, as if it was pornography. She knew she was being weird.

But the sad, dark eyes, framed by the kerchief and the little hoop earrings, called to Sugar, saying, "I get it; I know just how it is." Marvella seemed like a best friend or sister, the only person Sugar felt connected to these days.

"Thanks, Miss Nancy." Sugar took a sip from the cup, enjoying the adultness of drinking coffee, though she used so much cream and sweetener that hers could barely be called coffee.

"You know to just call me plain old Nancy. I don't put on regal airs or demand a special title. No sirree, Bob. That would be for Her Majesty downstairs."

"Okay, plain old Nancy," Sugar said, thinking herself pretty funny.

"Queen Darlene is the only royalty around here. She thinks she is, anyway." Miss Nancy didn't say anything about Sugar calling her "plain old Nancy." Miss Nancy didn't really understand other people's jokes.

Her Majesty downstairs, Queen Darlene, was Miss Nancy's daughter-in-law.

"Shannon? You up yet? Because the girls sure are!" Miss Darlene hollered just then, from her bedroom down on the second floor.

Miss Nancy felt that Sugar would have better chances in life with a name that didn't belong on a grocery list, so she'd introduced Sugar to everyone as "Shannon."

Miss Nancy also disapproved of her little granddaughters' names, Cherokee and Cheyenne. She'd said, "Let's just hope Queen Darlene doesn't have another one. She's liable to name it Flathead or Kickapoo."

Now, upon hearing Queen Darlene's voice, Miss Nancy inhaled, a deep staccato breath through her nose, the same organ she seemed to speak through. A nose-mouth, a mouth-nose. A face cloaca!

Sugar and her friends knew lots of hysterical words. Cloaca, frotteurism, coprolalia, smegma. Her last group of friends, that is. Or maybe it was the friend group before that.

"Yes ma'am. Coming!" Sugar called. She rushed to the little bathroom down the hall. A few minutes later, she emerged, wearing the required bright orange vest, over her jean shorts and Fleetwood Mac t-shirt.

The vest had a big yellow bird applique on the back. Warden Ella was as into bird themes as Miss Nancy was into sex crimes.

Queen Darlene was into staying in bed. Sugar rushed down the two flights of stairs, wondering if unbalanced interests came with age.

According to the daily chore list, today's breakfast would be eggs, bacon and grits. Breakfasts alternated between cooking days and cold cereal days. "What would you like, Miss… I mean, Nancy?" Even after three weeks here, Sugar still had a hard time calling an adult by only her first name.

"I'll just have whatever you're making them." Miss Nancy nodded toward her granddaughters.

"You want grits with it?" Sugar teased.

Miss Nancy oinked like a pig, which cheered Sugar up. Miss Nancy claimed grits were pig slop. In her view, high class people: (1) Were from up north, and (2) Did not eat grits.

Later, Sugar started the dishwasher. Then she started the washing machine. Miss Nancy painted her nails at the kitchen table, in Avon Pink Toffee nail enamel.

"You may use my nail polishes any time, dear," Miss Nancy croaked, probably noticing that Sugar was watching so enviously she was about to cry. "It's all in our bathroom. Just help yourself."

"Oh, wow. Thanks! Want some more bacon or anything?"

"No thank you, dear. I raised my child myself, without the services of a live-in maid, so I'm not used to being waited on. Or laying around all day while my husband goes to work." Miss Nancy glared up at the ceiling.

Miss Nancy's husband died a few years ago and then she moved down here from some small town near Des Moines, to live with her son and his family. She worked part-time as a receptionist at the men's jail, probably in hopes of meeting a real live sex murderer.

She seemed to like Sugar, though. In fact, Miss Nancy was the one who'd hired Sugar from Miss Ella's home jail, after Queen Darlene's last live-in helper quit.

Miss Nancy had said, "Since my daughter-in-law insists on having a slave, may as well at least get one for half price." That earned her a dirty look from Miss Ella.

Sugar wasn't a slave, though. She was paid $25 a week, plus room and board. But her checks came from the county, not from Miss Nancy's family. Sugar wasn't sure how it all worked.

Miss Nancy helped her open a savings account and showed her how to deposit half of each check into it.

"Give me a runaway over a thief or an addict any day," Miss Nancy liked to say. That, and "I don't believe a young person runs away from home without a good reason to."

Sugar hadn't run away from home, though, but only from a group home. She'd been trying to *get* home. Or to what she remembered as home, anyway. Miss Krell's house, her placement from age seven or eight until she was about eleven, was her favorite. She didn't know why she was sent away, or if old Miss Krell was even still alive.

Sugar just thought she'd take her chances since her placement at that time was so crappy. Come to find out, trying to go somewhere less crappy was a crime.

She didn't get far. Then, since she was fourteen and old enough to get a worker's permit, she was given the option of going to Miss Ella's home jail. From there, she'd been rented out as live-in help, in order to "learn valuable life skills in a wholesome family environment."

Sugar picked this deal, because her only other option was the juvenile detention center.

"Fourteen!" Miss Nancy had shrieked, after she finally thought to ask Sugar her age. "Why, that is child slavery, pure and simple."

"Almost fifteen," Sugar said, worried that Miss Nancy would take her back to Miss Ella's. Then Sugar would have to start all over again. And who knew where she might get sent the next time.

But Miss Nancy just did her nose-mouth snort, then went back to reading her latest library book, Jack the Ripper and Other Sex Killers of Victorian England.

Sugar set out the basket of coloring books and fat pre-school crayons for the girls, then sat down to fold laundry at the coffee table. This load mostly belonged to Miss Nancy, who didn't always seem to mind receiving child slave services.

Miss Nancy drove Sugar down Beach Drive, headed to the jail for Sugar's monthly check-in. They pulled into the driveway. It was a highly unorthodox jail. Miss Nancy did not approve.

"You wouldn't see *this* up north. No sirree, Bob," Miss Nancy said. Queen Darlene had told Sugar privately that she didn't know what the old bag was so conceited about, since there was nothing in Iowa but corn and cow flops, with Nancy being the biggest cow flop of all.

Sugar considered this now. She felt it was always best to consider all perspectives. She felt like defending the jail and Miss Ella now, even though she didn't like them.

People who were born on the island, BOIs, often stuck together against people from other places, just on principle.

The cells here were big go-go dancer cages that Miss Ella had hung from the ceiling instead of using regular jail cells. They looked like big bird cages, which went with Miss Ella's bird theme of teaching jail birds to fly right.

The women's jail could only hold six women. The place was usually full nowadays, with the growing population of the Isla Ajaja. The space limitations were why Miss Ella had started hiring out inmates.

As Miss Ella had explained to Miss Nancy, "That, and because it teaches 'em something.

What these gals need is job skills and job references--- and the chance to learn how a decent family operates. Now, some of them have had all that but plenty of 'em ain't. And that's why they're here."

For those who remained on site, Miss Nancy thought the place was run like a kindergarten. She asked Sugar if the inmates were retarded.

"I don't think so. I think Miss Ella used to run a daycare here though," Sugar said, through gritted teeth.

"Okay girls, who wants to show us their family dance?" Miss Ella said to the inmates, who were seated at the two end-to-end picnic tables.

Miss Nancy said, "Excuse me. We're here for Shan--- Sugar Mason's monthly check-in."

We'll get to that in a while, Miz Quinn," Miss Ella said, "Sugar, why don't you have a seat. Now girls, the family dance ain't just for girls who have got in trouble or who come from a family with troubles. Everybody has a family dance.

Miz Quinn here, for example, has a family dance. Miz Quinn, would you come on up here, please?"

Miss Nancy breathed in sharply, through her rattly nose. "Who, me?" she said, wild-eyed, as if she'd just been ordered to pull down her pants.

Miss Ella smiled and waved her fingers, like "Come on, let's move it." Sugar perched on the edge of the picnic table bench, eager to see what would come next. To her surprise, Miss Nancy went to the front of the room as instructed.

Miss Ella said, "Girls, this here family dance, or whatever it was originally called, comes from a smart and famous lady named Virginia Satir. Now, our family changes with time. So, when it's your turn, you can show the dance of the family you come from, or the dance of your family now, if that's different. Miz Quinn, which do you pick?"

"I really can't dance. I'm sure one of these girls will do it better," Miss Nancy said, trying again to get out of it.

"That's okay, it ain't really dancing. Do you want to do your family now or the one you come from? Or was there another family arrangement in between them two that calls to you the most right now?"

"I suppose I'll pick the family I have now." Miss Nancy slumped.

"Alrighty. And who do you consider to be in your family now?"

My son, Michael. He's an accountant." She always said it like he was a king or something. Though come to think of it, he should be a king, seeing as how he was married to Queen Darlene.

"Alrighty. Who else is in your family?"

Well, my two little granddaughters, they're three and four... And their mother. And Sugar."

"Good job! Now, Sugar, you come up here by Miz Quinn. And then we'll have Miz Quinn pick out some other girls to act as her son, his wife, and her granddaughters."

Miss Nancy picked out her actors. She picked the ugliest girl there to act as the beautiful Queen Darlene.

Under Miss Ella's direction, Miss Nancy positioned everyone, according to how she saw her family members' places in relation to each other.

"Darlene" stood on top of a picnic table that had been dragged over for that purpose, far above everyone else. "Michael" (Miss Nancy's son) kneeled on the picnic table's bench, reaching up toward his wife, Darlene, like he was begging.

Miss Nancy herself also kneeled on the bench, next to her son, reaching out to him. The little girls were positioned under the picnic table for some reason. Miss Nancy put Sugar right next to her, on the side Michael wasn't on.

She put her arm around Sugar.

Then Miss Ella made Miss Nancy have them all start moving, in the way that best showed their true positions within the family. That was the "family dance."

"Darlene" spun in a circle, high above everyone else, and not connected to anyone else.

"Michael," Miss Nancy's son, ran around and around the picnic table, trying to catch his wife's notice as she spun.

Miss Nancy, acting as herself, followed after Michael, with her hand out, as if trying to connect with him and also trying to stop the crazy circling. The little girls wandered about, only paying attention to each other. Through it all, Miss Nancy kept Sugar right with her, tucked under her arm.

Sugar watched, interested, from her position under Miss Nancy's arm. This family dance seemed correct to her, though she'd never thought of it that way.

Only she didn't know Miss Nancy considered her to be such a close tie. She hadn't known that at all.

"Now, freeze!" Miss Ella said, and all the actors stood still. Miss Ella just let the moment stand, a dramatic ending.

Miss Nancy said, "Lord have mercy. I just realized my daughter-in-law is just like my mother was."

The room went silent for a minute. Then everyone clapped, led by Miss Ella.

On the way home, Miss Nancy treated Sugar to an ice cream cone at the Island Breeze Dairy Freeze. They were quiet, each lost in her own thoughts.

When Sugar tried to picture what her family dance would be, she moved Miss Nancy onto the stage in her mind. Marvella, the girl in the local history book, was there too, a face on a page, floating around in the air.

The tension between Miss Nancy and Queen Darlene exploded. Sugar was drying the girls off after their bath when she heard a commotion coming from Queen Darlene's bedroom down the hall.

Miss Nancy yelled, "I've had enough of you. Enough! Get your lazy fanny up out of that bed right now. Or I'll get you up myself, by God."

Yelling by Queen Darlene followed, then a loud thump.

Not wanting to miss the excitement, Sugar told the girls to go wait for her in their bedroom. She rushed down the hall. Queen Darlene was on the floor and Miss Nancy was trying to slide her out of the bedroom, by one ankle and one wrist. Sugar found it all delightful, a break from the usual humdrum drudgery.

Queen Darlene kicked her free leg wildly. It was unclear what her goal was with that, but she didn't have no drawers on.

Sugar inspected with interest. She couldn't believe that two babies had come out of there. She'd thought ladies would be gaping wide open forevermore after practically shitting a watermelon, like a pouch with no drawstring.

But no, it just looked regular. Sugar wondered if this was a geometry problem, something she'd have been able to figure out if she'd stayed in school. The thought was so moronic that it made her laugh.

"Get out of my house, you old witch!" Queen Darlene shrieked at Miss Nancy. "All you've ever wanted was to break up my marriage."

"Well, that's true," said Miss Nancy said nasally, still tugging on Queen Darlene's limbs but not as vigorously.

Queen Darlene noticed Sugar, who'd moved over to more closely view the bare crotch on display. "What the hell are you staring at? You think this is funny, do you? Well, you can get out, too. Get out!" she screeched. "Oh, just fuck all y'all." She flopped back and lay still as death.

Miss Nancy let go of her. Queen Darlene lay on the floor and the lamp was on its side next to her, having been knocked over in the tussle. The scene looked like the aftermath of one of Miss Nancy's beloved sex crime stories.

"Come on, Shannon," Miss Nancy said, nose in the air. "Pack up what you can carry. I'll have Michael bring the rest."

Stunned, Sugar did as she was told. All her belongings fit into the big duffel bag she'd arrived with, so she packed everything up, then carefully tucked in her black and white photo of Marvella.

Miss Nancy was already in the car when Sugar came outside. The little girls chased each other around the front yard, still naked.

"Bye-bye. Y'all be sweet," Sugar called to them.

The next monthly check-in at the jail was quick. Miss Ella didn't ask if there had been any changes, and neither Miss Nancy or Sugar wanted to rock that boat, so they didn't say anything either.

On the way back to their new apartment, Miss Nancy pulled into the Ocean Breeze Dairy Freeze again. They walked along the beach with their treats.

Miss Nancy was awed at the big white pelicans. "Look at that," she croaked happily. "Would you just look at that."

"Huh. I didn't think you liked anything about Ajaja," Sugar said, fishing to find out if Miss Nancy would be sticking around for long.

"Well, honey, I do and I don't. It's beautiful here. But a big change is hard, at my age. Michael is all the family I have left, though. There's nothing for me in Iowa anymore."

"Oh, Wow. Sorry. I hear you about big changes." Sugar thought change might be harder for somebody like Miss Nancy, though.

Miss Nancy didn't seem to like new things. She ranted about bikinis and rock music like they'd just now dropped down on Earth and scared off all the wildlife. And she always picked the plain vanilla ice cream.

Sugar popped the last piece of her pink coconut ice cream cone into her mouth, wondering if something was wrong with Miss Nancy's mouth that kept it from being able to taste flavors right. Maybe something to do with that nose-mouth problem. That would explain Miss Nancy always picking the plain vanilla.

Sugar's job was better now, in a way. Miss Nancy didn't make her wear Ella's Rockin' Robins vest, for one thing. That thing was mortifying out in public. People stared and whispered.

Queen Darlene had seemed to get a kick out of it. At the grocery store, they'd always run into people Miss Darlene knew, who would make a fuss about how charitable Miss Darlene was to give a troubled girl a chance. They probably didn't know Miss Darlene stayed in bed half the day while Sugar did all the work.

And at Miss Darlene and Mister Michael's house, there was an ongoing list of things to do. There was no such thing as "being finished." Here, there was only a small apartment and one old lady to deal with. Sugar got her housework and cooking done in a couple of hours a day.

Then she had another hour or so for her required study, and that was all.

But the apartment was tiny, only one bedroom. Sugar had to sleep on the sofa. And Miss Nancy talked constantly. She croaked on and on about Queen Darlene, about how much better everything was in Iowa, about her indigestion, insomnia and numb feet. There was nowhere for Sugar to go, to get away from her.

Soon, Miss Nancy's shifts at the men's jail couldn't come soon enough.

One evening after Miss Nancy left for work, Sugar decided to try out the apartment swimming pool. She'd seen some other teenagers hanging out there. She dug out her bathing suit, grabbed a bath towel and slipped out of the apartment.

Miss Nancy said she wasn't mad. But suddenly, Sugar couldn't seem to do anything right. The towels weren't folded right. Fold them in thirds, not in halves. That's just lazy! The coffee mugs weren't clean enough. They need to be bleached when they get stained; pay attention! And the room air conditioner was set too low. Would you like to pay the bill for *keeping this place as cold as a refrigerator?* (Sugar hadn't touched the air conditioner controls).

Sugar told her new friends not to knock on the door because it set Miss Nancy off. Besides, after Miss Nancy met a new friend of Sugar's, she usually found a reason to ban Sugar from hanging out with them.

For example, Marnie wore a string bikini and Sheila had bleached hair, which qualified them both as streetwalkers, according to Miss Nancy. And Lionel was black. "I'm not prejudice, myself," Miss Nancy said. "I just don't want you getting a reputation under my watch, that's all."

Sugar was so starved for the company of other teens that she would have welcomed anyone, from the squarest kid to the most deviant. But Sugar herself was the worst among this group.

She was a ninth-grade dropout on parole.

One of the kids who knocked on the door was Gloria, the most goody-goody girl in the world. Miss Nancy didn't outright ban Sugar from Gloria. But she let Sugar know that she highly disapproved, on the grounds that Gloria was fat and would encourage poor eating habits.

Sugar and Lionel laughed about it, in the pool.

"What time does Miss Nancy get home tonight?" Lionel said.

"A little after ten."

"Cool, that's three more hours. Come up to my place. My mama won't be home 'til late."

Chills came over Sugar, like she always felt when she got a chance like this, equal parts thrill and fear. She wasn't like other kids. Any misstep could dump her whole life upside down.

"I don't know. I have to wash my hair," she said, then hated herself for saying something so dumb. To lighten up the moment, she mussed Lionel's afro. She said, "Boing-boing. It's spongey!" Then she swam away, expecting him to come after her and roughhouse.

But when she came up for air, he was just standing there, stiff. He got out of the pool and left.

"What's his problem?" Marnie said.

"I don't know. I'm going to his place in a while." Sugar didn't want to make a big thing out of whatever had just happened. Especially not to Marnie, who Sugar didn't completely trust.

An hour later, Sugar knocked on Lionel's door, freshly showered and wearing her favorite red flower print top. She also wore a kerchief and small hoop earrings, like Marvella in the picture. Sugar greeted Lionel with her brightest smile.

He sort of smiled back and waved her in. She was disappointed to see that Marnie and Sheila were there.

Sugar had fun anyway. They made popcorn. Then they made prank phone calls to one of Marnie's teachers from the last school year, then to a crabby neighbor lady. Both victims hung up as soon as they were asked if their refrigerator was running, but it was fun anyway.

Then they called Gloria to come over. Sugar liked Gloria but she wasn't above laughing at her a little with the others.

Gloria showed up with her Bible. She brought along a little straight pin, too. She'd stick the pin in between the Bible pages randomly. Then she'd read whatever passage it landed on.

She made them take turns. That was Gloria's idea of a wild time.

Everyone but Gloria howled when Marnie's passage instructed her not to covet her neighbor's ass.

"Tell my fortune next!" Sugar said.

Gloria went pale. She said, "Oh, no. Fortune-telling is satanic. This is holy."

"Oh, sorry," Sugar said. She was dang good at putting her foot in her mouth with this group. Then she caught Marnie's eye and knew from the mean gleam that Gloria's reaction would be hilariously re-enacted later. That made her feel better.

Sugar's Bible passage was nothing special. But Lionel stood behind her chair and rubbed Sugar's shoulders, which was good fortune enough for her. "Loosen up, champ," he kept saying, which made no sense to Sugar but she still liked it.

At 9:45, Sugar said, "Well y'all, I better go, before I turn into a pumpkin."

When she got home, Miss Nancy was already there. Sugar's heart did a double beat. Miss Nancy never said that Sugar was not allowed to go anywhere. It was more like Sugar knew she better step carefully or Miss Nancy would be mad but not admit it outright.

But all Miss Nancy said was, "Look who I brought home!"

It was a puppy. A tiny, adorable, black fur ball.

For a shining moment, Sugar thought the puppy was for her, for her upcoming birthday.

Giving her a puppy was just like what a mother would do. Sugar gushed, "Oh, wow. Oh, my gosh. Thank you, thank you, Nancy! I don't even know what to say---"

Miss Nancy swooped the miniature puppy up and carried it into the kitchen. She said, "Let's see what mummy has for her doggeenie doggette. Let's see if mommy has some yum-yums for her little puppy-wuppy girl."

It wasn't Miss Nancy's fault. Sugar had just misunderstood. She went out through the sliding door and sat down on the balcony to hide her hot face.

Miss Nancy checked out a book of baby names on their next library trip. After much study, she named the puppy Nyx, for the Greek goddess of night.

Miss Nancy no longer got mad when Sugar hung out at the pool. Sugar's friends could even knock on the door. Miss Nancy's focus had shifted from Sugar to the dog. Nyx was often found hiding, under the bed, under the sofa or even behind the toilet. Miss Nancy was too much for the dog, too.

Sugar was thrilled to get to hang out with the other kids though, even after Lionel decided he wanted to be Sheila's boyfriend instead of Sugar's.

It was a carefree summer of hanging out at the swimming pool, at the apartment of whoever's parents weren't home, the mall and the bowling alley.

Sugar didn't even mind taking her turns at getting jabbed. Gloria's straight pin Bible readings somehow morphed into them all walking around with a straight pin and sticking each other with it when they got the chance.

Sugar thought it was most likely Marnie's idea, since Marnie was definitely the meanest of their little group.

Sugar wasn't surprised, though, when Miss Nancy decided Sugar's services were no longer required, and that the apartment really wasn't big enough for two people anyway.

Back at Miss Ella's jail, Sugar lay on the mat, idly rocking her cage back and forth and looking at her picture of Marvella, not caring who thought it was weird. *I guess you're my whole family now,* she thought.

Miss Ella called them all to the picnic tables for one of her activities. Sugar, still sad about Miss Nancy dumping her, thought about refusing to participate.

But Miss Ella spread a big boxful of wallpaper sample squares on the tables and Sugar got curious. Maybe they were going to do an art project, like something with decoupage. Sugar had always wanted to try decoupage.

Miss Ella said, "Okay, girls. Pick out the square that calls to you the most. Take your time because you only get one."

Sugar felt a pang of nerves. She didn't like not knowing what was coming next. The ladies were nicer to her than they were to each other, she guessed because she was so young. But she still didn't want to look foolish in front of them.

"I see some of y'all are taking this serious. And that's good! But don't worry. Just pick the one you like the most, that's all. As the saying goes, it ain't rocket science."

Sugar finally took a square that had lacy pink and red hearts all over it.

After all six inmates had a wallpaper square, Miss Ella made them take turns talking about it. When Miss Ella asked who wanted to go first, Sugar volunteered, just to get it over with. She said her square reminded her of Valentine's Day, which she always used to look forward to. It was true. They'd have candy and cupcakes and valentines at school, and the decorations were pretty. It was a fun and special day.

She was relieved that she got to keep her turn short. The ladies just nodded in their friendly way. A big woman with a mop of curly red hair said the small blue oval shapes on her square reminded her of the pills she used to take. That led to a big discussion about addictions.

The next lady's square reminded her of her little boy's bedspread at home, which started another discussion, about the women's kids, then about their childhoods.

These ladies could even turn a dang wallpaper sample into a soap opera.

Sugar wished they could go outside and play dodge ball or something for a change, instead of endlessly blabbing on about their problems. Miss Ella's was really just one more place where Sugar didn't fit in.

She wondered if Marvella had felt the same way at the poorhouse. Nah, they'd probably just worked all the time when they weren't busy suffering from scabies or yellow fever or tuberculosis. The poorhouse book had let her know for sure that things could be worse.

When the wallpaper squares were finally put away and the six inmates were eating supper at the picnic tables, Miss Ella said, ' Your mama is coming to visit in a while, Sugar."

Sugar groaned, then felt bad when Miss Ella gave her a hard look. Sugar focused on her meatloaf and mashed potatoes and shrugged off the ladies' questions. They'd all see, soon enough.

Sugar heard her before she saw her. "Sa-gah, Sa-gah! I lub you, Sa-gah!" She came lumbering in and accidentally knocked her own thick glasses off while assaulting Sugar with an overly tight hug and slobbery kisses.

"Hello. How are you?" Sugar said politely. She looked at the woman who accompanied her mother, hoping for rescue.

"Now Mindy, remember what we said about shaking hands?" the grandmotherly helper said, pulling Sugar's mother back.

Sugar was glad "Three's Company" was on the TV, so she could at least pretend the other inmates were watching it, instead of getting an eyeful of the ruckus Sugar's mother made with her loudness, largeness and bowl haircut.

"Look, Sugar, your mama made this for you," Miss Ella said. She handed Sugar a lump of hardened clay with holes poked into it, painted yellow with some bare spots. It looked like something Cherokee or Cheyenne would have made, back at Queen Darlene's house.

"Oh. That's pretty. Thank you," Sugar said. She settled in dutifully for her visit. Sugar didn't really know this mentally handicapped woman or feel a connection with her. She just had to pretend like she did for an hour every year or so, with these awkward, embarrassing visits.

But somewhere between playing pattycake and letting her mother win at "Go Fish," Sugar started feeling calm and content, the way she'd often felt with Queen Darlene's little girls.

The break from analyzing and gossiping and other adult complications was refreshing. All was simple and in-the-moment with small children and Sugar's mother.

Miss Ella said, "Oh, I'm sorry. I forgot to introduce y'all. Sugar, this nice lady is Miz Fontaine, the director of your mama's group home. Now, we've worked out a deal where Miz Fontaine will be your new sponsor and the group home will be your new placement. Sugar, you are going to go live with your mama!"

Miss Ella announced this like she was awarding Sugar a big prize. The other inmates clapped and said "Yay!" and "Oh, how nice!"

Sugar was too shocked to respond. She didn't trust her voice. And she didn't even know why she was on the verge of bursting into tears. But she would not cry in front of everyone and be the focus of even more cheerful pity.

She nodded politely, then made a beeline for the restroom, to get a minute alone.

February, 1984

Sugar's position as an aide at the Sunshine Women's Home suited her. Sugar's mother living here made it a "family placement," as far as the county was concerned.

But. of course, it was not a family home; it was a business. Which meant Sugar's role was necessary, clearly defined, and could reasonably be expected to last.

With foster homes and work homes, her position was always iffy and usually short-lived. She was on the outer edge of whatever family she was placed with, and subject to their whims.

For the first time since Miss Krell's, when she'd been too little to understand the ways of the world anyway, Sugar felt like she was home.

Miss Fontaine told her on her first day, several months ago, that it would be best if Sugar called her mother by her mother's first name, "Mindy" and kept the fact that she was Mindy's daughter to herself.

"The girls," as the thirty-six adult female residents were called, easily got jealous and got their feelings hurt. Staff were instructed not to play favorites.

Sugar was relieved. The thought of being expected to play daughter, to a toddler-like mother who she barely knew, had overwhelmed her. Not to mention the lurid questions having a mentally handicapped mother brought up for the nosy entertainment of other staff members.

Now, fortunately, the issue would just be left alone. Her mother was, more or less, just another resident. Sugar was fond of her in the same way she was fond of many of the other "girls." It was a pleasantly distant fondness, without emotional demands.

Sugar and Mindy shared the same last name but none of the other employees seemed to make the connection. Sugar and another aide, Katie Thomason, had just finished supervising the lunch clean-up, and were setting up Valentine's Day projects for the girls.

The project was big, fluffy flowers made with colorful tissue paper and coat hangers. Miss Fontaine liked activities that resulted in something the girls could put in their rooms or wear. It was good public relations, for the parents and caseworkers to see evidence of the girls receiving extra attention.

Katie said, "For the level A's, let's cut the tissue paper to cover the stems but then put it aside for the girls to put on. For the level B's, let's go ahead and cover the stems for them." The girls were roughly categorized into two groups, A and B, according to their ability level.

"Sounds good," Sugar said, straightening out metal hangers with a pair of pliers. Of the staff, Katie was closest to Sugar's age but still quite a bit older, in her early twenties and married.

Only Sugar and Miss Fontaine lived here, though most of the others worked twenty-four or forty-eight hour shifts.

Katie said, "Hey, what are you doing Saturday night? Are you off?"

"Um, why?" Sugar said, suspicious.

"I just thought you and my husband's little brother might like each other. We could double date, go see *Ghostbusters,* then get a pizza or something. No big deal."

Sugar felt the chill she got whenever something exciting came up. For her, fun had always come mixed with a fear of being sent away.

But nobody here had any confusing or unspoken expectations of her; she was just a worker. Nobody cared if she went out. She said, "I don't know. What's he like?"

Katie was already going through her purse, digging out photos. "He's almost seventeen. And you're fifteen, right? He's a super nice guy. He's shy."

"I'm fifteen and a half," Sugar said, looking at the Polaroids Katie handed her. He was just sort of regular looking. Medium height, with brownish hair. Great teeth, though, straight and white. She said, "Okay, I'll go."

For the rest of the week, Sugar dwelled on the upcoming date. She tried out different hairstyles, different eyeshadow colors and different outfits. She went through many scenarios in her mind of what he might say or and how she should respond. She was a wreck.

At 7:00 pm on Saturday night, Katie and her husband pulled up, with Joel in the back seat. Sugar waited on a bench outside the Sunshine Women's Home. She was showered, perfumed, blow-dried, made-up, be-jeweled and dressed in a bright red sweater and new jeans.

Her date got out and opened the car door for her. *A gentleman.* "Hi," she said brightly, getting in.

Sugar had rehearsed so well that the date went smoothly. Joel briefly dropped his lit cigarette in the car and blushed about it, which was how she knew he liked her. His nervousness made her confident.

She hoped he'd call.

He did. The next time, the two of them went out alone.

September was a good month for Sugar. She turned sixteen. And she was released from the custody of the juvenile justice system as an emancipated adult, since she had a job and a place to live. Miss Fontaine kept her on the same as before but increased her pay, from the $25 per week the county paid her to $80 per week.

She and Joel reached their six-month anniversary of going steady. They celebrated with a candlelight dinner at Ramone's Seafood, a fancy place overlooking the bay. He presented her with a promise ring, a thin gold band with a tiny, twinkling diamond. Sugar felt quite grown up wearing it.

Then they went to Joel's family's fishing shack, where they went all the way for the first time. When Katie heard about it, she promptly dragged Sugar to Planned Parenthood to get on the pill.

Back at the Sunshine Women's Home, Katie said, "You don't want to be like my sister Linda. She got pregnant and the guy dumped her. And my mama kicked her out of the house. Things just kept going downhill from there."

"Huh. I didn't know you had a sister. Where is she now?" Sugar said.

"Oh, she and her husband Chuck own a bar in town. They're loaded. They live in a big bayfront house over in Sunset Reef.

"Wow," Sugar said "That's amazing. Maybe I *should* get knocked up too, then." "Don't even say it." Katie jokingly swatted Sugar's bottom, which made the residents in the day room shriek with laughter.

Most of the girls there were on the pill, though they didn't know it. It was just given to them each morning, along with their vitamins. Some of them went out into the community, for simple jobs and for visits home and such. Miss Fontaine wasn't taking any chances.

"Well, I gotta go now. See ya tomorrow," Katie said.

"Yep, see you. And thanks," Sugar said, as Katie headed for the door.

Sugar was off duty, but she'd taken over some of the office work from Miss Fontaine and the filing was backed up from some time ago. Miss Fontaine hated to file. Sugar grabbed a Coke from the kitchen and headed for the office. She may as well get a jump on the filing so tomorrow would be easier.

In the office, on top of the desk, was a manila file folder. It was labelled "Mindy Ann Mason."

Sugar's breath caught in her throat. Had Miss Fontaine left it out on purpose, wanting Sugar to see it? She pushed it aside and started filing the big stack of papers next to her. She stopped filing a couple of times, picked up Mindy's file, then put it down again.

All Sugar knew of her father was that he had taken advantage of a retarded girl. Sugar wasn't one of those people who was drawn to dark secrets, like Miss Nancy, and some of her co-workers who always turned on the afternoon soap operas in the day room.

Sugar had had enough mess and chaos in her life, she didn't feel drawn to looking for more. She'd probably never have gone looking for the information in the folder on her own. But when it was put right in front of her... She opened it.

The folder was thick. There were a few photos of
Mindy at various ages, getting heavier and heavier through
time. Beneath that was a stack of medical records. Then a page
with contact information for Mindy's parents. *Mindy's
parents.* Sugar never thought about Mindy having parents.
Mindy's parents, Sugar's grandparents, had lived right here on
the island.

Sugar wondered if Mindy ever went on home visits or
if her parents still lived around here, or if they were even still
alive. She wrote down some notes and put them in her purse.

Sugar's birth certificate did not have a father listed but
there were notes about Sugar's "probable" father, as he was
called, in Miss Fontaine's loopy cursive handwriting.

Mindy had lived with her parents until age 24, when
she was placed here at the Sunshine Women's Home. Under
the space that asked for the reason, it said "Parents unable to
control her." Mindy did throw a tantrum now and then, and it
could take several staff members to restrain her.

Shortly after being placed here, Mindy got pregnant by
a boy who worked with the yard crew. His name was Leo
Worth, and he was seventeen years old at the time. His blood
type matched up, and both he and Mindy admitted that they'd
"had relations."

Sugar was surprised to read that they'd wanted to get
married, but then she thought the boy was probably just trying
to stay out of legal trouble. The marriage wasn't allowed,
since Mindy was not considered mentally competent. Then
Sugar learned that the boy was only a little better off than
Mindy. His IQ was listed as in the "borderline retarded" range.

Sugar found herself wiping her eyes. In the little
thought she'd ever given to her father, she'd assumed he was a
creep, the type of criminal that Miss Nancy would be out of
her head with interest about, a sex pervert. But Sugar's
parents, however handicapped they were, had been in love. It
was really kind of sweet, in a sad way.

Someone was trying to turn the doorknob now. Sugar
stuffed everything back into the folder, then unlocked the
door. It was only one of the girls, one with Down Syndrome,
who had a tendency to wander. "Go on back to the day room,

honey," Sugar said, and watched to be sure the girl headed in the right direction.

Sugar went up to her bedroom, scolding herself for being a mushy marshmallow.

Whatever had happened was long ago and she was here now, and that was all there was to it. But the revelations wore her out, even if they were about things she hadn't thought she cared about in the slightest. She lay down on her bed and fell into a deep, dreamless sleep.

Things took a turn one night at Katie's, while the two couples were playing Monopoly and eating potato chips out of Katie's new wooden chip and dip set that she'd gotten as a wedding gift. Sugar suddenly fell out of love with Joel.

Well, the feeling had been coming on for a while, but Sugar hadn't recognized it for what it was, until now. As she landed on Baltic Avenue, she suddenly felt claustrophobic, like she couldn't take another minute of being in a committed relationship. "It's too hot in here," she said. "I'm gonna step outside for a minute."

"Are you all right?" Katie said. "You don't feel nauseated, do you?" Katie was trying to get pregnant, so she read pregnancy into everything.

"No, just overly warm. Don't worry."

"I'll come with you," Joel said, a gentleman as always.

"No, thanks. But would you take my next turn for me, if I'm not back by then?" She'd learned it was better to redirect Joel than argue with him. Joel liked to help.

There was a breeze out front and the palm trees swayed above the Christmas lights on the small houses. Sugar cooled down and could breathe again. Then she felt great, being outdoors, with so much open space, and cool air flowing all around her. She had to stop herself from twirling down the driveway and out into the street.

Sugar was glad Katie was so happy, she really was. Katie was pleased as punch to be a newlywed, in the small depression era home she and her husband had just bought. Katie arranged and rearranged her secondhand furniture and the doilies with the dog figurines on them, and proudly displayed her wedding gifts. There was the gleaming new toaster on the kitchen counter (four slots!), the large blue and green ceramic lighter and ashtray set on the coffee table, the lime-colored bathroom towel set with a matching shower curtain.

But it might have been Katie who'd brought on this last straw, earlier, when she asked if Sugar thought she, Katie, ought to get drapes for her living room window (which was currently covered with a bedsheet) or if blinds and a valance would be enough. And then, what color?

Forest green would go well, but then so would tan. Sugar got tired of talking about it after ten or twenty minutes.

As Katie rolled the dice then, Sugar had started feeling terrible for her. What lay ahead for Katie was endless years of boring housecleaning while her husband cut the boring grass.

Then she'd have to do some boring ironing and think about trying a boring new ground beef recipe for dinner. All that, and only that, over and over and over again.

Sugar and Joel were headed the same way, that much was clear. Joel with his mild good manners and the routine they'd already fallen into themselves, with the little diamond on her finger promising a real wedding set soon.

Joel was about to graduate early from high school and start working full-time at his father's hardware store. Earlier that night, he had talked to Sugar about a little house that was for sale down the block from here.

If Sugar went back inside now, she'd burst into flames, then blast off through the ceiling and, perhaps, to the moon. Or perhaps just politely suffocate and die. Certain that she would sound crazy if she tried to express any of this, she called Joel outside to tell him she felt like she may be coming down with something. She asked him to take her home.

Sugar got out of it the chicken way. After she was granted the two weeks off work that she had coming to her, she broke up with Joel over the phone, hands and voice shaking.

Joel rushed straight over to the Sunshine Women's Home to "talk about it" (she knew he would) but by then she was already on the bus to the mall, to hide out.

Miss Fontaine noticed a change in the air and asked Sugar what in the world was going on. Sugar told her. Miss Fontaine said, "Well, of course. Goodness. You're only sixteen years old," as if that settled everything.

In a way, it did settle everything, in Sugar's mind. Sugar had just never thought about it like that.

It wasn't long before Katie reported that Joel was dating someone new. The new girl was part of Katie's couples' get-togethers now.

Sugar hung out with Miss Fontaine. One night they were watching a corny country TV show that had a zillion people dancing at a hoe-down and shouting things Sugar didn't understand, like "Cotton Eye Joe!" The dancers locked arms, skipped a little, then moved on.

With a start, Sugar recognized it. An endless reel with new people, leaving the old ones behind, that was her family dance. "Do-si-do!" she yelled, then laughed at how moronic it sounded. Miss Fontaine gave her a strange look but Sugar didn't feel like explaining.

The Yule Tide

Winter, 1986

Linda Thomason watched from the back seat of the patrol car as Sheriff Earl Schmidt pulled into the driveway of a big one-story house. The place was on several acres of land, with no nearby neighbors. Linda would be quite alarmed to be taken to this isolated house instead of a real detention center, if she hadn't already heard about Ella Schmidt's kooky home jail, with the big bird cages instead of jail cells.

Words were painted on the wall above the TV: *I Know Why the Caged Bird Sings by Maya Angelou.* What did that mean? Was it something about jailhouse snitches? Linda had heard snitching called "singing" before. Well, whatever was painted on the wall, her main feeling now was relief.

The place looked like something out of a horror flick at first glance, but it was really kind of cozy. You could lay down on the sleeping mat inside the cage and rock yourself to sleep, just like you could if you were in a hammock, because the cages were ceiling mounted. When Linda was instructed to join the other five inmates at the picnic tables in the middle of the big room, she had the strange sensation of being in a daycare for grown-ups.

Miss Ella made them write sentences while they waited for dinner. Some of the ladies protested when Ella handed them their stapled together notebook paper, with the sentence each inmate had to copy written on the front page.

"Girls, hush," Miss Ella said. "I didn't say nothing about what you done or ain't done. I just told you to write the sentence that I gave each of you, a thousand times. That won't hurt you none, whether you're guilty or innocent. Now do what I said. Number your sentences. And this won't be finished today anyhow so take the time to write neatly. Or else I'll make all y'all start over."

Miss Ella walked around the room, looking over their shoulders. Linda started copying the sentence Miss Ella had written at the top of her page. "I will not commit murder."

By sentence number twenty-five, she was itching to know what the others had to write. She tried to peek at the packet of the pudgy gal on her left, but Pudge snatched up her packet and glared. "Sorry," Linda said.

At around sentence number fifty, she tried again. She dropped her pen on the floor, on her right side, then got out of her seat to retrieve it. When she peered up, pen in hand, the tall, thin girl sitting there popped her eyes at Linda. Then Beanpole flipped her packet over and slapped it down on the picnic table. Linda gave up.

Linda went back to her own place at the table but it was too late. The middle-aged Black woman across from her had snatched up Linda's packet. The woman shrieked, "Oh my god. She the girl that kill her own mama! I seen it on the news."

Linda said, "No, I didn't." But no one seemed to believe her.

The place didn't seem cozy anymore. Linda picked up her packet and took it into her cage. She lay on her mat, facing the wall. She was careful not to rock the cage. Better not to do the slightest thing that might call any more attention to herself. The other girls chattered and whooped about her. They didn't understand. "Murder" was way too strong a word.

Nobody tried to understand Linda's side at all. Even her own sister had turned on her, and it wasn't the first time for that, either. Linda never forgot about the last time Katie snitched on her big time. Linda had her reasons, when she let that Jaci girl take off with Linda's kid.

Everyone acted as if letting your kid go on an extended camping trip with a friend was a crime or something. That was years ago but now Linda realized that Katie was a rat, period. And a rat would always be a rat.

As soon as Katie had seen the body bag on the news channel, she went running to the sheriff, motorboating her mouth about how Mama had once made her, Katie, a sun dress with the same fabric the body bag was made from. Katie claimed she recognized the strawberry print. Mama had made Katie a dress, that was true. But had Mama ever made me a dress for Linda? Hell no, she did not.

Then Chuck had the nerve to blab his flappy-floppy lips on the news, too. He said, "I'm not too surprised, really." Then he made a sad face. Everybody knew Chuck had been the bad one in their relationship, not Linda. And the thing with her kid all those years ago, that was as much Chuck's fault as it was hers anyway. Of course, Chuck made sure he was interviewed right in front of the sign for his business, Barnacles Bar. Linda's biggest lifetime mistake was being too forgiving. She should never have kept disloyal rats like Katie and Chuck in her life, once they showed their true colors.

A Few Months Earlier

Linda walked into the bar's office, looking for a box of cocktail picks. She nearly plowed into Chuck, whose back was to the door. Chuck didn't seem to notice that she'd come in.

He was too busy making out with Marjorie, a forty-ish, sun-damaged and whiskey-skinny bartender.

The other employees called Marjorie "the husk" when she wasn't around. Linda wasn't sure if it was because of Marjorie's raspy cigarette voice, her maddeningly slow drink mixing speed, or just because she seemed kind of burnt out and ready for the compost pile.

"Uh," Chuck said. "Uh."

Linda called, "You're fired," at Marjorie's bony back as the woman slunk out of the room, though Linda wasn't really authorized to fire anyone. Then Linda shoved Chuck out, too. She shut the door in his face and locked it.

Linda knew she was supposed to feel jealous. But it was *Marjorie*. She took a deep breath to calm the confusion in her mind. The phone was still ringing, so she answered it. "Barnacles Bar, may I help you?"

"I've got some bad news, sis."

"Who's calling, please?"

"Um, Katie. Your sister? Anyhow, listen. Mama's in the hospital and it's bad. I just saw her. Can you come?"

Linda's first feeling was relief at getting to leave the bar. You didn't leave right before the Saturday night rush without a damn good reason. Just catching your guy cheating on you didn't seem like enough, especially if your guy was Chuck. In fact, Chuck was the only one who left whenever he felt like it. But then, he owned the place. "Be right there," Linda told her sister.

Boswell had beat Mama up again. Linda already figured that, without even asking. Mama had strict rules that she applied to everyone except Boswell and herself. Besides making excuses for Boswell when he beat her, Mama claimed that she and Boswell were married "in God's eyes." But Linda had had to make Mama think she was legally married to Chuck or risk getting kicked out of the will again.

Chuck. Oh, Linda was tired of him. It had been a long time since those wild nights back in the old trailer. Then they'd started the business and got the house and felt like they were making it big in life. Sometime after that, Linda started to wonder if Chuck just kept her around as a trophy, to make other guys envious. Or because of what she did for him, working harder at his bar than he did, and for so little in return.

Chuck was not the prize he seemed to think he was, not anymore. He got the shakes, wet the bed and went on icky crying jags, and the years had only made it all worse. He was completely, unappealingly, out of control of himself. Except when it came to hogging all the money and dodging Linda's attempts to get him to marry her. Then, as the saying went, he was crazy like a fox.

For the first few weeks after Mama came home from the hospital, Linda, Katie and a couple of hired helpers took turns staying with her. Then they realized a more permanent arrangement would be needed, because Mama was not coming back from the head injury inflicted by Boswell.

Linda volunteered to move in with Mama. It would be an easy path out of her dead-end relationship with Chuck and she was ready for it. She grabbed a trash bag and started counting outfits to toss into it. Five days' worth was good enough for now. Five tops, five pairs of jeans, five bras and pairs of underwear. She'd move the rest of her stuff out later, a little bit at a time.

Before driving away, she took a long look at the pretty bayfront place she'd been so thrilled to move into with Chuck, in the Sunset Reef development. She'd had such high hopes then.

Mama could handle basics like feeding herself, after a plate of food was put in front of her, and using the restroom herself, thank god. But if you didn't watch her, she was liable to turn on the stove and forget about it, leave the bath water running, or wander out of the house and not remember where she was. One day, Katie found her at the neighbor's door, asking for a sandwich. After that, they'd had childproof locks installed at the tops of the doors.

Mama seemed at about the same mental age as Linda's daughter was when she'd been adopted out, about three and a half years old. It crossed Linda's mind that maybe this was her punishment. But she wasn't the type to dwell on things. That would only drive you insane.

Linda wasn't used to having so much time on her hands. She kept an eye on Mama from a distance and Mama didn't come looking for her company, either. Mama would have screaming fits, though. But then, there had always been either silence or screaming between her and Mama.

Mama got especially wound up at night. She'd accuse Linda of stealing her things. The bottle of Evening in Paris cologne that had sat on Mama's dresser years ago. Mama's pink slippers, which were right there on Mama's feet at the time. "Not those pink slippers! My other pink slippers!" Mama yelled. She even accused Linda of hiding their dog, Smoky, who'd been put down when Linda was in elementary school.

Once in a while, Linda messed with Mama. She hid the pink slippers. She told Mama that the dog's name wasn't Smoky, it was Boswell. The real Boswell had run off while Mama was in the hospital, and he hadn't been back. So that was one good thing that had come of it all.

Linda found a big box of paperbacks in a closet, science fiction and true crime. She guessed they'd belonged to Boswell because she didn't recall Mama ever reading, unless it was something practical, like a cookbook.

Mama started waking up at night screaming, too. She seemed miserable, a lot of the time.

There was one true crime book where a woman had put her husband down over time, with antifreeze. She'd mix it into his morning orange juice.

Katie came over a couple of times a week to visit or give Linda a break.

Linda said, "So, at that women's nursing home you work at, do they ever put them down?"

"It's not a nursing home. It's a group home for mentally disabled women."

"Same difference. But do they do ever put them down? You know, like a veterinarian does? Like if they're too miserable or sick and won't get better?"

"Uh, no. Are you crazy?"

"Uh, no. Are *you* crazy?"

Katie sighed, then went back to blabbing on about her new sewing machine. Linda's little sister Katie had started acting like she was the big sister. Linda didn't like it.

Linda was bent over, getting a fresh nightgown out of Mama's bottom dresser drawer, like she did every night after she had Mama brush her teeth. Suddenly, Linda slammed hard into the dresser, headfirst. The old woman had kicked her, right in the ass! The old woman had an enthusiastic smile on her face.

The next morning, Linda put a little antifreeze in the old woman's orange juice. Just a spoonful. If anything, it would probably just calm her down some, Linda reasoned.

"Do you know the combination to the safe?" Linda said, on Katie's next visit. Katie was unpacking some bags she'd brought in from her car.

"Uh, yeah. I do. Why? Look here, I thought we could sew Christmas stockings. We could use my new sewing machine. I brought it with me. It's in my trunk. Want to?"

"Okay, I guess so. I want to see what's in the safe, though. We need to find Mama's financial records. You know, it's what you do in a situation like this."

Katie wrote the combination down on a slip of paper. "Here it is. We can go through whatever's there, later on."

Katie had been given the combination to the safe, while she, Linda, the oldest, had not. Katie had always been the favorite.

"I bought stuff for five stockings. For Mama, us two and both of our husbands."

Linda just nodded. Katie had gotten quite conceited about her boring marriage. She'd be even worse if she knew Linda was never married after all and didn't even have a man now.

Linda had already had Chuck bring her the rest of her stuff. She'd told him she never knew what she'd need since she might have to be here for a while. So, could she just have it all until she could come back.

Chuck didn't argue. He told her that the husk had taken over Linda's job as bar manager. He said it was just until Linda came back.

That was two weeks ago and neither of them had called the other since. It was like they both knew it was over but pretended it wasn't. It just seemed easier that way.

The sisters spent the afternoon making the Christmas stockings, after sitting Mama down in front of the soap operas on TV, with a plate of Christmas cookies. The sewing machine was fairly easy to use. Katie left it there when she went home. She said she wanted to do more projects together after Christmas.

Linda opened the safe. Inside, there was a life insurance policy for $100,000. She also found the deed to the house. Mama had liked to brag that it was paid off. Linda and Katie already had access to the checking and savings accounts. They withdrew money from those to keep the household running. The money came from Mama's pension from the county.

If half of everything Mama had was Linda's, Linda could start over. She could have a nice life. She wanted to open her own business. She certainly had the skills for it, after running Chuck's bar for him. She'd start out small, maybe a take-out pizza place, or even just an ice cream stand.

The old woman's yelling cut into Linda's daydreams. The old woman was carrying on about how someone stole her car. Linda took her out into the garage to see the car. It was right there in the garage. But you could never prove anything to Mama. Then she just screamed that Linda had made the thief bring the car back as a trick. She started rocking and holding her head then, one of her headaches. Linda gave her some pain pills. The old woman was so very miserable. And she wouldn't be getting any better.

Linda found a bolt of fabric in the closet. It was cute, strawberries on a pink background. She used Katie's sewing

machine to make a large, cute, rectangular bag, about six feet
long by three feet wide.

The next week, Linda called Katie at about ten in the
morning. Katie and her husband were supposed to come over
at noon to help fix Christmas dinner. But Linda decided not to
wait until then to tell them the news. "Mama's gone," she said.

"What do you mean she's "gone?""

"When I woke up, she wasn't here. I walked all over
the neighborhood, then knocked on doors. I drove around after
that. I can't find her. Do you think we should call the police?"

"Yes! No. I don't know. I'll be right there."

It was going to be such a long day. And Linda was so
tired already. "Okay," Linda said. "Merry Christmas."

The Daily News
December 27, 1986
Human Remains Found

A woman's body was discovered on the beach this
morning by snowbirds Don and Dolores Mitchell of Nauvoo,
Illinois. Mr. Mitchell reports that the couple left their travel
trailer just after sunrise to stroll on the beach with their
morning coffee, as is their winter habit. The body was in a bag
made of pink fabric with a strawberry print. Mrs. Mitchell said
she thought at first it might have been one of those pink
dolphins, she'd read about somewhere, washed ashore.

The deceased woman has been identified as Betty Lou
Thomason, 52 years old, a lifelong resident of the Isla Ajaja.
She had recently been diagnosed with brain damage due to
head trauma. She was under the care of her daughter, Linda
Thomason, 29.

Mrs. Thomason was reported missing on Christmas
Day. According to the authorities, her body had likely been in
the water for two or three days, until it washed up with the tide

166

this morning. Please call the Isla Ajaja Sheriff's Department if you have any information.

Mr. Mitchell said he and his wife plan to return to Nauvoo immediately and didn't expect to return. "This island just ain't the same place it used to be," he said.

Linda asked the sheriff to grab something she could cover her face with, since he'd cuffed her hands behind her back. The reporters' cameras were already going, flashing through the window like fireworks on the Fourth of July.

Unfortunately, what the sheriff grabbed was what was left of the pink strawberry print fabric. Linda didn't understand why Mama had bought so much of it. Later news reports would call her a psychopath who wore the pink strawberry print fabric over her head to mock the victim.

As the sheriff led her to his waiting patrol car, Linda barely noticed the throng of busybodies, crowding around and shouting questions. She was thinking about Katie, and even Chuck. Linda, who had been a good friend to everyone, had nobody now. How easily people would throw you away.

Little Luxuries

Spring, 1990

Earl brought our kid sister Emma to the jail this time, but sometimes she comes in on her own, when she knows she done wrong. Or maybe it's more when she's scared or lonesome. Who knows how that brain of hers works. She's got her a job as a maid at the motel in town and they give her a good deal on a room there. But if you ask me, a motel room ain't no home. I don't like that place anyhow, ever since my friend Venice Jenson got herself mixed up in drugs and died there. It's really gone downhill.

Emma might show up any time of the day or night and hop right into an open cage. If all the cages are full, she'll grab a coupla blankets off the shelf and lay down under the picnic tables in the center of the room. Earl and I call her "Otis" after that drunkard on the Andy Griffith show who always turns hisself in to sleep at the Mayberry jail.

Of course, the other girls here love seeing that the sheriff and the warden have a jailbird in our very own family, like it proves we're no better than they are. Not that we ever said we was, but it's still an embarrassment, to be sure. But there's eight of us Schmidt kids and the rest of us is all right, more or less. Emma's the baby. Earl thinks she's just spoiled. But she never was quite right. Even as a toddler, she'd bang her head on the wall or floor until it bruised, if you didn't catch her and put a pillow in the way. Sometimes she'd just stare, up at the corner ceiling, with her head at a funny angle. But back then, we girls helped with the housework and the little kids. The boys had outside chores. So he probably just don't remember little Emma like I do.

Earl rolls his eyes, like "here we go again," and hands me a sack containing the items Emma stole this time: bubble bath that was packaged to look like a bottle of pink champagne. A bottle of perfume with a birthstone sealed inside the bottle (Emma picked the one with a fake emerald; her birthday's in May, so she got that right, at least). A little enameled jewelry box shaped like a piano, and a pair of earrings shaped like little red fox faces.

Emma steals the silliest things. Well, no, she steals things that are real pretty looking. She don't know cheap junk from Chanel though, she only cares if something is bright and shiny. She takes fancy looking things, not necessities. She can't afford to pay for no extras, that's for sure. Earl and I have to help her out with just her basics half the time, things like bread, peanut butter and dish soap. Her stealing problem might just be because she has a childish mind and can't afford cute stuff she wants but don't need. That is, if you can make sense out of a disordered mind at all.

I arrange the stolen items on my desk and take a Polaroid of them for Emma's file. Then I put the stolen goods all back in the sack and give it back to Earl, to take back to the store. That's our usual procedure. I said, "I thought they didn't let her in the dime store no more."

"They had a new girl working the register. I reckon she didn't recognize Otis," Earl said.

"All right. I got her." Emma had already grabbed some blankets and made herself a little bed under the picnic tables. She looked a little too comfortable to me, considering what she just done. "Wait, I been thinking of an idea. Can you help me a sec?"

Earl shrugs. "Sure. What do you need?"

"Bring her on up here, would you? I'll be right back."

I have a whole stack of books on self-help activities but I don't rule out using plain old common sense, or old school discipline, either. Heck, even a dog knows to stop a bad behavior after it gets a good whack for it a few times. I go out to the garage and grab the hammer.

"Okay, Earl. Let's see, she's left-handed, so hold her left hand down on the desk for me. Hold down the back of her hand, not her fingers."

He did, and I hammered Emma's fingers hard a few times.

Emma started caterwauling like I just chopped off her dang head. Earl's eyes got real big, which got me to laughing. On the serious side of it though, Emma is at high risk of the judge sentencing her to state prison, due to her being a repeat offender. Surely, a few smashed fingers was better than that.

I told my baby sister, "The next time you think about taking something that don't belong to you, remember this. Because if you do that again, I'm gonna do this again."

The other girls started calling out comments, first defending Emma and yelling about how my punishment was cruel. But they soon turned to whistling at Earl instead and rocking their cages so they clanked into each other. When one of the girls starts yowling, it sets the rest of them off, just like a group of babies in a daycare.

And of course, they practically lose their minds whenever a male comes around anyhow. I've been making up some activities based on the Emily Post etiquette book. I'm here to tell you, these girls need 'em. The home training is sorely lacking, with most of them.

I get some sheets down and start covering the cages. They calm down when you cover up their cages, when there's nothing to look at.

My brother Earl says he wants to talk to me outside. That means he don't want the girls to hear whatever it is he has to say.

Out on the porch, he hems and haws. I say, "What is it? I've gotta get supper started."

He says, "This is serious. You might want to sit down." He gestures at the porch swing, which I take a seat on.

He says, "I know something that I ain't supposed to know and I'd lose my job for tipping you off about it. So, what I've got to say is strictly between you, me and the fence post. Got it?"

I feel my breath catching. I say, "Got it." Whatever's going on, it don't sound good.

He says, "From what I was told, this facility has been under investigation for a while now, behind the scenes, by the state. Are you okay, sis?"

I put my hand up, letting him know to hold up a minute. I need to catch my breath.

He sits on the porch swing next to me and lights a Marlboro. He offers me one and I take it, which don't make much sense when I can't catch my breath as it is. But him offering me something feels like caring, which I surely need right now.

I say, "What are they investigating this facility for?" though I have a pretty good idea of the answer to that question.

"There have been reports of, ah, unusual rehabilitation methods. Which they are calling possible cruel and unusual punishment. The term "torture" has been used."

I just shake my head. If they know so much, how come their state prisons are so full of repeat offenders that they have to keep building new prisons to hold 'em all? I say, "My methods work."

Earl just nods. We finish our cigarettes, looking out over the scrubby, sandy yard.

August 25, 1990
The Daily News

Isla Ajaja Residents--- Evacuate Now!
Hurricane Dee is expected to hit the upper Texas coast early
Monday morning. This is a very dangerous storm. Winds may
hit category three strength before landfall. Please evacuate
from the barrier islands as soon as possible. For those who
need assistance, busses will be leaving from the parking lot of
the Isla Ajaja City Hall beginning at noon today, headed for
shelters north of Houston.

I've got the girls getting themselves fed, showered and
packed while I try to figure out what in the world to do next.
The girls seem giddy at the idea of taking a road trip. I'm sure
they're planning all kinds of mischief. Oh, this is a mess. I
lock the front door and start heading toward my quarters to
pack, when someone knocks.

It's Earl. He says, "Step outside a minute, sis." I do,
and I see a thick dark line all across the sky, way off on the
horizon. Hurricane Dee is on the way, for sure.

I toss my hands up in the air. "How in the world am I
gonna handle six wild girls out on the road?"

Earl looks around. He lowers his voice. "Sis, with the
state, it's gonna be serious. They're talking about several
felony charges."

I start pacing and practically panting. I can't breathe
when I get this upset. I say, "It ain't much different than what
kids get, a spanking or being sent to their room without dinner,
or whatever. Only more so, to fit far bigger wrongs than kids
do."

"They're fixing to come down hard on you, sis, starting
with the cages."

"The cages are cute!"

"It ain't up to me."

"Well, what the heck do you want me to do about that
right now? Are you trying to make me have a heart attack?
There's a hurricane coming, you know."

He says, "The timing couldn't be any better. That's why I'm here right now."

I can tell by the tone of Earl's voice that he has gone into full-on big brother mode. I say, "I'm listening."

"Good. You ain't been indicted yet, so you are still free to move about freely. Now pack a suitcase and get on out of here, right now. Leave the cages and the front door unlocked here. Drive to Canada. And don't come back until I tell you to."

"Why should I leave everything unlocked?"

He says, "So these ladies can find their way to safety. And so at least some of them might not be found and therefore, cain't show up in court to testify against you. You got any better ideas?"

I shake my head, so relieved to have a way out of such horrific trouble that I can't even speak. I give Earl a big hug, then I go inside to hurry up and get the heck out of town. It don't seem fair at all though, how everything could go so wrong, when I tried so hard.

Lady Land

June, 2016

    The Friday night GateFest, also known as the HateFest, picks up, as people start getting off work and arriving. I stand around with the other women, inside the barred gates to Lady Land. My husband Dan is here too, dressed like a woman. I say, "I'm not staying for long. My head is killing me."

    Dan says, "I got you." That's one of his new, "with-it" phrases. He pulls a bottle of ibuprofen out of his purse.

I snatch the bottle and swallow a pill, with no water. I don't thank him, because I didn't want to come to the gates in the first place.

We watch with the other women inside the gates, as the men jostle into position, outside the gates. The men yell horrible, misogynistic things. "Incels," I believe they're called these days.

I wish they'd all spontaneously combust from the heat of their own repulsive rage. Or at least just go home. I don't know why anyone would want to interact with them.

A few men carry bunches of roses or boxes of candy though, as if wanting to make amends with a Lady Land woman, or maybe they're hoping to attract one in the first place.

Besides "incel," my grown children and internet searches have taught me other modern words. For example, "greysexuals," who are not old people having sex, as one might guess, but just people who aren't very into sex.

Another one is "demisexual." That is just a person who's only attracted to someone after they get to know them. In the olden days, would have just said they were slow to warm up or not into casual sex. Or maybe we'd just say they were a little shy, and not mention sex at all.

When I got around to looking up "pansexual," I thought of an online video I somehow accidentally saw once, where a big turtle tried to mate with a pan. I believe it was upside-down wok.

The new labels mostly just seem to me like a way for young people to feel like they're exotic when they're ordinary, but what do I know.

Spectators gather on picnic blankets on the grass, beyond the raging, highly unappealing males. The blanket people eat sandwiches they brought from home or burgers purchased from the roving vendors. A reporter walks around, snapping photos and asking people questions.

I hear my daughter Lindsey, out there somewhere, playing her guitar and singing. She plays songs like "Only Women Bleed" and "I am Woman, Hear me Roar." It makes me cringe. I say to Dan, "I wish the girl would at least do that here on the Lady Land side of the gates, where it's safe."

The whole scene has a vibe somewhere between a picnic, a carnival, and a political rally. And a loony bin, obviously, though I've been told you shouldn't say "loony bin" anymore. Or "retarded," either. Nor even "diet," because now you're only supposed to try to be healthy, not skinny.

If I could play the guitar, I'd play that old Beatles song, "Yesterday." I'd play it over and over and over again.

Dan says, for the third time, "Gail, hon, this is a huge phenomenon. It's in the news all over the country!"

I don't care about these obnoxious Friday night gender wars at the gates, or the whole women-only concept of Lady Land either, to be honest. I only live here because we happened to find an affordable home and business set-up behind the Lady Land gates. And we had to do something, after the hurricane washed away our former life last September.

Lady Land was originally just a little shopping strip with a beauty spa, a couple of women's clothing stores and a tea room, stuff like that.

The Lady Land name was meant to pay homage to the female ghosts that supposedly had inhabited the old fortune-telling parlor that burned down, the old Jenson shack. In other words, it was a gimmick somebody used to make a lot of money. It still is, if you ask me.

I still hear about Jaci Jenson once in a while, the girl who grew up in that old fortune- telling shack. I remember her. I can't imagine having eight grown kids like she does now, though. Hers were all adopted as older children, too. The woman's a saint. My two are plenty for me. Too much, sometimes.

I used to come out here to Lady Land through the years, as it was building up. I'd have a girls' day with Lindsey. We'd eat crepes, see a chick flick, and maybe get our nails done.

Men didn't pay much attention when the Lady Land shopping center owners stopped letting them in. Most of them didn't want to go to any girly shops anyway.

But Lady Land somehow evolved into an entire incorporated, women-only town. Well, that's not *completely* true. After all, my husband and my son both live here now.

They had to jump through some hoops to get in though, and they have to keep jumping through hoops to be allowed to stay. For one thing, they have to present as women whenever they're out in public, inside the Lady Land gates.

Dan is talking to a gaggle of women now, complaining about how he can't find talcum powder. Apparently, it's been taken off the market. He wanted some to dull the unnatural shine on his synthetic wigs. I step away from him, embarrassed.

Today Dan wears a wild jungle print dress. He's doing that thing I hate, where he flaps his hand and says, "Girrrrl." I grab his flappy hand and pull him away from our neighbors.

I mean to distract him with small talk. But what comes out of my mouth is, "Can I go home now?"

He does his new pouty mouth thing, which is especially unsettling to me when his mouth is covered in red lipstick. At first, I found the men's dressing up rule kind of hilarious. Big Dan, dressed like a woman! That was before I realized that Dan likes it. It's not funny anymore.

It's getting louder now. Females, males and a few indeterminates, argue across the gate, name-calling and even reciting gender-based poetry at each other, aggressively.

Some of them hold up signs: "You Women Want it Both Ways." "Males Are 95% of the Prison Population for a Reason." Some of the signs are much more vulgar than that.

Dan blows his noisemaker, one of the ones that are for the females to blow. It's called a "growler" and makes a ridiculous low-pitched fart noise.

"Would you stop?" I say. It's loud in my ear.

He makes that lipsticked, pouty-kissy mouth again and I have to turn away. Noisemakers can be heard from both sides of the gates, adding to the chaos. The men's whistles are called "chirpers." They make an annoyingly high-pitched, bleating noise.

The whistles are meant to mock male or female voices.

I want to heat up some of my leftover mac and cheese and turn on re-runs of *The Golden Girls*. I'm about to leave when I spot my new daughter-in-law, Nicole, strolling around outside the gates with Lindsey. My daughter and daughter-in-law act like Siamese twins lately, if "Siamese twins" is still a permissible term to use.

I nudge Dan. "Look, Nicole is trying to make some money, for a change." He just shrugs.

The male's noisemakers fill a box that hangs around Nicole's neck by a cord. She calls, "Chirpers, five bucks! Get your chirp-chirp-chirpers here guys, cash or credit card!"

She and Lindsey chat between Nicole's calls for customers. Those two are always talking about what feminists they are, yet here Nicole is selling whistles for men to mock women with.

The atmosphere is getting louder and uglier. I feel the tension rising, like something big and bad is likely to happen. I say, "Oh, I wish those silly girls would just get over here, inside the gates." I catch the girls' notice and motion for them to come over. So does Dan.

They wave to us, then shake their heads in unison, *no*.

I say, "Well, we tried. See you at home." I locate our golf cart and drive the short distance to our house, forcing unpleasant thoughts out of my mind. Instead, I decide to add a nice bubble bath to my plans for the night.

I said something my daughter didn't like and now she isn't speaking to me. I simply told Lindsey that I didn't think it was safe for her to go out to the bars alone, let alone wearing an outfit that was so skimpy it looked like a negligee.

How in the world could that translate to me saying it's a woman's fault if she's assaulted? That's not what I said.

She also said she knew people at the bars so she wouldn't be alone, but that is not a solid plan at all. Those "people," whoever they are, may or may not even be there. Naturally, she went anyway.

Well, I guess I'll be picking up this load for my store on my own then, if I can work out a deal with the lady who owns the stuff. Of course, Lindsey will probably expect a break on her already very low rent when it's due, even though she refuses to work whenever she gets mad at me.

I called Nicole to see if she wanted to come help me and make some money today but she didn't answer her phone and didn't call me back. I see her car over there in front of their place. She's most likely either sneakily siding with Lindsey against me or just being lazy. Probably both.

I thought it was perfect that our new shop and house compound came with the two little guesthouses. I liked the idea of being able to help our kids out with super low rent and get to have them nearby, too. But I'm starting to think it was a mistake.

We got along better when we lived a little farther apart, well, with Lindsey, anyway. My son Leo is more easy-going and he doesn't work with Dan and I anyway, except once in a while. He manages a hotel in town.

If we didn't all live right on top of each other, I wouldn't know so much about Lindsey's activities in the first place, or when my daughter-in-law was avoiding me. I'd be happier that way.

Dan calls while I'm on the way to town and says his dentist appointment is done, so he'll meet me at the house I'm headed to.

When I get to the house, the deceased woman's daughter answers the door. I walk through the place with her, taking notes. She wants to sell nearly everything in the house. I figure up the quote and she accepts it right then. When Dan arrives, we start loading up my van. It will take a few trips.

The next day, Dan comes out of the garage with the new shop sign he's made for me. It says, "Back to the Future Resale Shop." My previous resale shop was called "The Secondhand Rose."

I worked there with my parents nearly my whole life, off and on, then the business transferred over to me completely when they both died, a few years back. The icing on that nasty cake was the big hurricane, coming in and sweeping everything away.

"It's beautiful," I say, about the sign. Dan's painted a little DeLorean next to the wording, like the time machine in the *Back to the Future* movie. It's probably some kind of infringement but I doubt anyone will care.

He says, "Thanks, darling. I'll put this up, then I'm going to run into town and get a new microwave."

"No. I mean, let's not. Not right now, okay?" I don't want a new microwave.

"Gail…"

I decide to change the subject. "If you feel like helping out, you could put another load of blankets in the wash. The guinea pigs need their dinner, too." I'm hosing down two dirt-caked bicycles.

When we buy out a whole house, there's a lot to do. Dan helps me a lot more now that he's retired but he didn't really want me to start up the business again in the first place.

I keep a few items for myself from this haul. I keep a Tupperware Jello mold. I haven't had a Jello salad in years. I also set aside a red rotary dial phone, like the one that was in my house growing up. I'll have to call the telephone company and see if I can get service for it.

Then there's a couch throw, made from crocheted granny squares. Every sofa used to have one of those tossed over the back of it. Oh, and the Heaven Sent perfume. Wow, a spray of that takes me right back to the good old days. My grandmother used to wear it.

Dan comes in, screws up his face. "Hon, you know it's 2016, right?" He is looking at my new-to-me hip hugger, bellbottom pants. He thinks I'm going back to the past too much, as a reaction to too much unwanted change.

"Well Dan, it was a simpler, sweeter time, so what's wrong with that? Remember how you'd carry that old guitar around and we'd have all those sing-alongs?"

"That was forty years ago," he says, as if it makes any difference

Whenever I walk into my vintage-decorated home, I feel lighter, more hopeful. Dr. Phil talks about having a "soft place to fall" on his show and this is definitely mine. I say, "I bet most husbands would appreciate having a wife who preferred to buy second hand."

He shrugs.

I start dinner: pork chops, canned corn and frozen Brussels sprouts. I cook everything on the stove, the old-fashioned way, no microwave.

Dan washes up for dinner. He comes to the table wearing fresh red lipstick. He is not required to wear lipstick inside the house. His earrings appear to go all the way through his ears.

"You got your ears pierced?" I say, flipping a porkchop onto his plate, nearly missing the plate.

He shrugs. He asks for extra corn.

We have the kids over for tacos and margaritas, for my new daughter-in-law Nicole's thirtieth birthday. Kids get married so late these days.

At least now there are no worries about the kids driving home after drinking, since they all live just right across the parking lot.

Lindsey is speaking to me again. The first thing she says is that she's a hundred dollars short on the rent and is that okay. She says it in the whiny baby voice she's started using when she wants something. I don't want to get into another argument with her already so I say all right, though it's really not all right.

She's wearing a pair of pajamas I recognize from the shop, pink with a bunny print, like it was made for a giant baby. It looks a bit insane but I don't say anything. It's too soon to risk another argument. She is very quiet tonight.

Nicole shows off the new ring Leo let her bully him into buying, I mean surprised her with, for her birthday. It is in that weird new style. There's a garnet on one side and a small diamond on the other side. Between the two mismatched gems is a big gap. The first thing the eye is drawn to is a gap, right in the middle of the finger. Why would anyone design a ring like that?

I say, "Wow. That's pretty!"

After everybody has assembled their tacos and I've passed around the Spanish rice and the refried beans, Nicole says, "I have an announcement to make." She's blushing. I squeal, involuntarily. Our first grandbaby. How exciting!

Nicole stands up and waits until we're all quiet. Then she says, "I am…"

"Yes?" I say, leaning forward, eager.

She says, "…bisexual."

I burst into shocked laughter. I mean, that *is* a little crude in front of her in-laws, but I have to admit, it was pretty funny. I wait politely for the real announcement about the baby.

Nicole sits down. She looks like she's about to cry.

Dan says, to her, "Okay! Thank you for sharing, my dear." He doesn't look at me.

Lindsey says, "Good for you." She pats Nicole's back and glares at me.

She was serious? Why would she say that? Who cares if she is bisexual, when she's married anyway. And why on earth would she feel the need to stand up and talk nasty at the dinner table, for crying out loud.

I try though, I really do. I say, all cheerful and hearty, "Well then, happy bi-day!" but nobody answers me.

I'm in the back room of the shop, still sorting the items from that house we bought out, when I hear the door chimes jingle.

I say, "Why, Miss Ella Schmidt! I haven't seen you in a coon's age! How've you been?"

Miss Ella used to run the women's jail but it was destroyed in a storm. Not this latest one, but the last really big one before that.

There were rumors about her being under investigation back then, but I never believed it. I can't imagine Miss Ella doing anything wrong. I can't believe anyone would take the word of a bunch of criminals over hers, in the first place.

Anyway, it was all a long time ago.

Ella said, "Can't complain too much. I got me a little practice over on Oleander Lane, you know. Come on by sometime! We can catch up."

"Will do. What kind of business you in now, Miss Ella?"

She hands me a business card.

"Oh my. So, is that like being a therapist, then?"

"Somethin' like that," she says.

I don't see any letters after her name that indicate any kind of official certifications, just "Ella Schmidt, Life Coach." Then again, anyone her age probably has some wisdom to pass along, even without any letters after their name. Even if they did used to be a jailhouse torturer, haha.

At dinner, Dan said, "Did Miss Ella come by today?"

I was wondering how he knew, then it clicked in my mind. Dan told her to come. When you're with someone for decades, you just know things, without even knowing how you know them. It could have been an unusual lilt of his voice at the end of a sentence, or a little motion of his eyes, that my sub-conscience picked up on. Who knew.

I said, "You think I need a life coach, huh?" He was reaching for the salt shaker but I snatched it and set it out of his grasp just to deprive him, as he deserved. "Going around town trash talking me, huh?"

He sighed, deeply, as if I was some big burden to him rather than practically his damn servant. He said, "The guinea pigs were the last straw."

So, I had bought a few guinea pigs, just like I had enjoyed as a child. And just like our kids had enjoyed as children, too.

Once, when I was a kid, we went to the zoo and there was a whole big room full of them that you could play with. It was such a delightful, magical day, that I never forgot it.

"Gail. There are two hundred and sixty-seven guinea-pigs."

"But I only bought a few!"

"I just thought you might talk to Miss Ella, since you won't talk to a therapist. The guinea pigs are just one more way this living in the past thing is going off the rails. That damn waterbed hurts my back."

"I didn't want that many guinea pigs. I told you; I just can't always tell the boys from the girls. Besides, Lindsey likes them too. She helps with them. It's okay."

"No, it's not okay. And Lindsey is not progressing in time as she should anymore, either," he said.

I start to argue, then look over at Lindsey, who is drinking out of a sippy cup. I think she just likes to do things to annoy her parents. Don't they all?

I do need to speak to her again about taking things from the shop without asking, though.

No doubt, that's where she got that sippy cup. But I like it better when she acts young than when she acts like a know-it-all with Nicole, or goes out looking like a streetwalker.

I say, "Young people try out different things. It's a normal part of finding themselves."

He shrugs. That shrugging thing is quite rude, really. "Oh, shut up, Ru Paul," I snip. I stomp off, to let him know I'm super mad about him talking about me behind my back. I go to the girl guinea pigs' bedroom and pet the precious little dears while they squeak and purr.

The next day, I'm arranging the newly washed clothes from our big haul, putting them on hangers, then placing the hangers on the racks, by size. I don't see Dan or Lindsey. I wonder what they're doing.

I find them in the boy guinea pigs' bedroom. They've got a system going where they carefully inspect each guinea pig's bottom, then make sure it's in the correct guinea pig bedroom for its sex.

Dan says, "Okay, you win this round, since I don't want to embarrass you and guinea pigs don't live all that long anyway. But this is it. The end. When they die off, they're gone. And I'll be watching."

Lindsey doesn't say anything. She just sucks her thumb.

"Oh, *fine*." I go back out to the shop and light a patchouli incense cone, in an adorable ceramic frog incense holder. Incense used to be so popular.

I'm secretly relieved that Dan's managing the guinea pig population, though I won't give him the satisfaction of saying so. I don't like things getting out of control, or being in a position where people could talk about me. I heard once that the fear of being the subject of gossip is especially strong in people who were raised in small towns. You could definitely consider the Isla Ajaja a small town, aside from all the tourists, who don't really count.

I wait on customers, then continue working after closing time, cleaning and organizing.

Finally, the haul from that house we cleared out is all in place. If I do ever go see Miss Ella, I'll ask her why she still works. I'd expect her to have retired long ago. She might just need the money. But also, work *is* a nice form of therapy. It is to me, at least.

When I finally go back into the house, I see that Lindsey has made dinner. If you could call peanut butter and jelly sandwiches with apple juice dinner. She's in "her" room now, the one she always sleeps in when she stays over here.

Dan says, "Lindsey wants to move in with us."

"What? Why? It can't be money. I mean, we're only charging her four hundred dollars a month for that guest house. Including utilities!"

He just shrugs. He's wearing lipstick again. I slip into the master bathroom, locate his lipstick and toss it into the bathroom trash.

We may not be normal but we can at least try to look like it, dammit.

By Thanksgiving, the guinea pig count is nearly cut in half, down to 142 from 267. Ten of them died of natural causes. Dan talked me into letting him take the newest litters around to give away to pet shops.

And I keep a half dozen for sale in the shop at all times. I charge five dollars apiece, just so people will stop and think before taking one home. It's embarrassing how out of control the breeding got.

Lindsey's taken over the care of those that still remain. She sweeps the linoleum floors of their bedrooms daily and puts down fresh hay, along with feeding and watering them. She's just like a little kid with them; she enjoys them so much.

She's also started sewing herself little matching short and top sets, with an old sewing machine I let her take from the shop. The clothes do look a bit childish, with fabric that has little hearts or ducks all over it. But her teaching herself to sew is great. That's a valuable life skill.

She lives with Dan and I now. Her guesthouse across the parking lot stands vacant.

Dan keeps harping on how my "running back to the past," as he rather rudely puts it, has rubbed off on Lindsey. But kids do tend to take longer to fully grow up these days, so I'm not worried about it.

I'm worried about Dan wearing lipstick. He got another tube of it and I snuck that one into the trash, too.

We are preparing for Thanksgiving dinner. The turkey's in the oven, and the rest of the fixings are in process. The Jello salad is chilling nicely in its Tupperware mold, in the fridge.

Nicole had asked if she and Leo could bring a friend. It seemed to me she could have asked to bring dessert or a side dish instead of a stranger to our family holiday dinner.

But I said okay. It's harder to say no to a daughter-in-law than it is to one of your own kids, and I think they all know it, too.

I had just flopped down in my big, comfy new-to-me papasan chair, when Nicole and Leo arrived, with a girl named "Roo." I'd seen the girl coming and going from Leo and Nicole's place but hadn't talked to her.

Roo said "cool," a lot and had her head partly shaved in some kind of design, tattoos going all the way up one arm, and a pierced nose. I went into my bedroom and hid my jewelry box high up on the closet shelf, behind some boxes.

As we ate, we went around the table and took turns saying what we were thankful for, as is our tradition. We said the usual things, that we were thankful for: Our family members and our health and all that. I added that I was thankful that the past year had seemed calmer, that it seemed we might finally have reached a new normal, after the hurricane.

Then I felt bad, because I realized we had left Nicole and her friend Roo for last, which was probably not polite. I tried to make up for it by clasping my hands together and smiling brightly at them, like I was just dying to know what they were thankful for.

Nicole and that weird Roo stood up. They held hands. I thought oh no, not another announcement.

It was another announcement. Nicole said, "I am thankful for our new wife, Ruth Elizabeth Brown, otherwise known as Roo."

I glared at Leo, who suddenly became highly fascinated with his mashed potatoes.

Nicole added, unnecessarily, "We are a throuple!"

Dan the traitor zoomed straight over and congratulated them. I sat there with a frozen smile on my face, hoping none of the neighbors knew that my son was a pervert.

Lindsey said, "Goody gumdrops." It wasn't clear if she was just doing her little kid talk or being sarcastic, or if it was just an unusual word choice.

Dan thought the childlike stuff had gotten worse, after that night she went out to the bars alone. He worried that something had happened to her.

I went into the kitchen to fetch more dinner rolls and weep. I heard Dan say to the family, "Just give her a little time. She'll get used to it."

Roo said, "Cool. We're doing us and she's just gonna have to get with the times."

No, actually, I don't.

The whole stupid fight started just because I said something was "groovy." I don't even remember what it was now, something on TV. Apparently, words like "groovy" are not acceptable to Dan. Only words like "throuple" and "lipstick" are acceptable to Dan.

Just then, Lindsey happened to come into the kitchen. She had a pacifier in her mouth, of all things.

Dan started yelling about that, and Dan hardly ever yells. I tried calm the situation down by trying to get him to see the bright side of things, so I told him that it could be worse.

That, for example, our daughter could have a cigarette in her mouth instead, like so many young people do. That would definitely be worse, wouldn't it?

Instead of seeing the bright side, he started yelling at me about the guinea pigs, even though that wasn't the topic and there are only 133 of them now anyway.

Dan slammed his fist down on the kitchen table, which he never does. He said me and Lindsey were both crazy. Then he stomped into the bedroom, grabbed a bunch of his dresses out of the closet and left with them. He left!

Dan thinks he deserves the right to re-create himself and so do our son and his two wives, no matter how upsetting or embarrassing that may be to me.

But Lindsey and I do not deserve that same right. See, that might upset and embarrass him, which is an entirely different matter to Dan.

He left three days ago. He's staying in the vacant guest house and visiting back and forth with Leo and his two wives, who do not wave to us now or even look our way. Lindsey and I just stay over here on our side of the parking lot.

Jaci Jenson came into the shop. Well, I'm sure she's got a different last name now. I came out of the back when I heard the door chimes jingle, and there she was. Old lady Jaci. Ha!

I couldn't believe Amara was with her, that baby Jaci stole years ago from Linda Thomason, as payback for Linda stealing Jaci's boyfriend.

Back before Dan and I were married, we'd hang out over at Linda's, where Jaci was staying. We'd all sing along to Dan's guitar.

I heard that Linda chick killed her own mother, then escaped from the jail. She always was a cold fish. Beautiful, but on the outside only. She'd look straight through you. It was creepy as all get out. I heard that look described in a book once as "the psychopath stare," and I thought of Linda Thomason right away.

Anyway, baby Amara is in her forties now and about to become a grandma! I didn't recognize her at all, seeing as how she was just a toddler the last time I did see her. When Jaci told me who Amara was, it tickled me to death and also made me want to burst into tears.

I think of these kinds of moments, where the old and the new violently collide right in your face, as "time warps." Then I thought of the time warp song from the old *Rocky Horror Picture Show* and figured I was losing my tiny mind.

I ran into the house and got Lindsey, so Jaci could see my grown up baby, too. Of course, I didn't mean that literally. I first made Lindsey change out of her unicorn print sunsuit and put on jeans and a grown-up top.

Jaci bought out about half the damn store. I tried to throw in a few free guinea pigs but she wouldn't take any. She said it's their family tradition to exchange secondhand gifts for Christmas. It sounded very intelligent to me, especially since her family must fill up a stadium by now, with all those kids marrying off and having kids of their own.

After they left, I was still kind of wound up from seeing Jaci. Seeing someone aged a few decades is like seeing a funhouse mirror in a horror flick, except it's real. Well, that's an exaggeration but it is a bit unsettling, to me at least.

I was straightening things up then, when I happened to look up and catch an image of myself in a big ornate mirror some lady had brought in on consignment. I saw the room behind me, full of old furniture, lamps and pictures, a room from the past.

At the forefront of it all was me, an old woman. Just like Jaci. Terribly, shockingly, old. Time stood still in here, as far as inanimate objects. But time hadn't stood still for me.

I had to have already known all the information I saw in that mirror. I had to have known I was nearly sixty years old. But still, it hit me like a punch in the gut, seeing myself in that mirror. See, the current version of myself didn't fit with this vintage room. A young me would fit with this vintage room.

I managed to flip the sign on the door to "closed" before breaking down into a crazy sobbing jag.

Since it doesn't look like we'll be having a family Christmas dinner for the first time ever, I try to cheer Lindsey up. She's taking it hard. But I wish she'd stop talking about how Santa Claus isn't coming. I have bought her some extra nice gifts, trying to make up for the mess our family is in, I suppose. Genuine pearl earrings. Two winter tops. And a Coach purse.

I also got her a giant bubble wand and the liquid bubbles to use with it. She swooned when she saw the commercial for it on TV, and who says bubbles are only for little kids anyway.

And I got her a coloring book, but it is specifically labelled as an "adult" coloring book and comes with markers instead of crayons.

Then I couldn't resist the adorable Hello Kitty desk set, since she starts school next month. She will be studying to become a pre-school teacher. Christmas is not the time to try to change someone.

I suggest getting out of the house, having a girls' day out. By the time I close up the shop, Lindsey is already waiting in the van. She is appropriately dressed like a grown-up girl.

We get our nails done, while sipping free fancy drinks at the posh nail salon in town. I have mulled wine and Lindsey has hot chocolate. I pick a Christmassy red glitter polish. Lindsey picks five pastel colors. When her nails are finished, they look like Jordan almonds.

I've forgotten that it's Friday. The Gatefest is just getting started. We go over to the gates because someone said a bake sale was going on over there and Lindsey is whining for cookies.

"Silent Night" plays through a loudspeaker, though it's pretty much drowned out by the chirper and growler whistles. A young man who is wearing a hat with horns on top screams, "Cunts!" over and over again.

As if in response, a young woman behind the gates strips. She spreads her legs wide, her feet high up against the gate bars. The men on the other side of the gate go wild.

Lindsey starts to cry. I don't blame her. What a disgusting display. I quickly buy a box of pretty Christmas cookies and we head home. This is no place for a child.

I've planned Christmas day to keep us busy. Lindsey helps me make a beef roast with gravy, mashed potatoes, green beans, and dinner rolls.

I keep Christmas music on most of the day. We open gifts after dinner. I don't say anything when Lindsey blows many gigantic bubbles inside the house, though the soap bubbles leave residue everywhere.

I look out across the parking lot now and then but I don't see any signs of life over there.

My son's car is gone. Maybe they all went somewhere together or maybe Dan is sitting over there in his guest house, all alone. I leave the front door open, with just the outer glass door shut, even though it's chilly out. If any of them want to come over, my door is open.

We have the Christmas cookies and hot drinks, then settle in to watch Christmas shows for the rest of the evening. Charlie Brown and Rudolph cartoons, then the more grown-up ones.

I shut the door.

I wait until the day after Christmas to tell Lindsey my plans. I've talked Miss Ella into coming to babysit her while I'm gone. I offered Ella a nice chunk of money and told her she is welcome to continue seeing her life coach clients here too. I have her come a day early to give Lindsey a chance to get used to her before I leave.

I return home ten days later, with a new face, a tight middle and high breasts. Lindsey cries when she sees me. I don't know if it's because my face is still swollen and bruised after the plastic surgery, or just because she missed me. A nurse's aide helps me get into bed.

Miss Ella says, "Well, I'm already packed up so I'll be getting out of your hair now."

"What? You're supposed to stay for two more weeks, remember?" I start to get out of bed, to continue my protest but the nurse's aide makes me lay back down. She starts reading my care instructions to Miss Ella, about my pain medications, diet, and so on.

Miss Ella cuts her off. "Tell her," she says, pointing at Lindsey, who is sitting on the edge of my bed, clutching a stuffed bunny.

I start to argue some more but the front door shuts. Miss Ella is gone.

Lindsey looks terrified. She begins sucking on the bunny's ears.

The nurse's aide shrugs, and starts reading the instructions to Lindsey, holding up various bottles of pills. "She needs this one every four hours, this one every two hours, and this one as needed for breakthrough pain. It's all written on in the instructions."

Lindsey sets the stuffed bunny down. She nods along with the instructions. The aide finishes, then says, "Call the number on the bottom of the page there, if she has any problems.

Any questions?"

Lindsey says, "Can I leave her alone, to go fill her prescriptions or pick up food?"

The aide says, "Only leave her for a half hour or less, for the next couple of days."

"Okay. Thanks, ma'am."

The aide looks from Lindsey to me like she's a bit confused at how the mentally disabled girl in the corner suddenly turned normal.

Dan came over twice that week for short periods of time while Lindsey ran errands. I pretended to be asleep.

Lindsey was a grown-up the whole time, from what I saw, and a pretty amazing one at that. She took care of everything: me, the household, the shop. She tucked the stuffed bunny in under the covers with me. It was like Lindsey got older when I got "younger." Or something like that. I don't know.

A month later, I still have to take it easy. Healing takes longer when you're older. But I have to say, I absolutely love my new appearance. I know I don't look twenty, but I don't think I look sixty anymore, either.

I had Lindsey move that big ornate mirror from the shop into the house. But then I had her return it to the shop, because I couldn't stop looking at myself. It started giving me the unmoored feeling of going too far again, getting out of control, like with the guinea pigs.

I was a little ticked off at Miss Ella, though. I decided to give her a call and a piece of my mind.

She answered the phone, "Ella Schmidt, life coach."

This is hard because I was raised not to talk back to my elders, as goofy as that sounds when that elder had just cheated me out of a lot money.

I said, "Hello, Ella," deliberately not saying "Miss" Ella. "Um, about that extra two weeks I paid you for, but then you left?" I'm cringing, even though I know I'm in the right. This is just so awkward. I'd definitely have just let it go, if it wasn't $2,000.

She tried to change the subject. She said, "How's that daughter of yours doing? Was she able to grow up and help you out?"

I accidentally slip into friendly conversation mode, because I'm puffed up with pride.

"Lindsey was amazing. You know that issue of childishness I told you about? Well, I didn't see any of it. She took care of me like a professional nurse, along with running the household and the shop. I was very pleasantly surprised. Now, she's back in school. She wants to be a pre-school teacher, you know."

Miss Ella says, "Then you got more than your money's worth. We're even." And she hung up the phone!

After Miss Ella hung up on me, apparently, she called Dan. Come to find out, she was talking to Dan, Lindsey and the throuple across the parking lot the whole time I was away.

I found this out after Dan showed up at my door. Lindsey and I had just finished cleaning up after supper and I was pouring us each a glass of wine when he knocked.

He stood in the entryway, holding a big clamp-on lamp. I waved him in, then called down the hall, "Lindsey! Your father's here."

He said, "Um, actually, I came to see you."

"Me?" I said, fluffing up my hair, a vain little habit I seem to have picked up after becoming $100,000 prettier.

"Yes. I mean, if you don't mind."

"No, I don't mind."

Dan asks Lindsey if she'd mind going over to the guest house for a while, so he could have a word with me in private.

After she leaves, I say, "Would you like a glass of Merlot? I just poured these for Lindsey and I."

"Sure," he says, and I invite him to sit down.

He says, "First of all, I know you're mad at Miss Ella and that you don't like anyone else in our business, which I understand I also want you to know that I bought you a box of chocolates, but I thought it would be presumptuous to bring them over, without knowing if you wanted that kind of attention from me anymore."

He takes a sip of wine and watches me, while I try not to bounce up and down with joy.

He wants me after all! I accidentally fluff my hair again. To my mortification, my new younger, cuter self adds on a goofy giggle.

Dan raises an eyebrow, like *Who are you?*

I say, "For future reference, I'll always accept chocolate. What's with the lamp, anyway?"

"Well, it was Miss Ella's idea. She's a smart old bird, by the way"

"That's one way to describe her."

"Oh well, no one's perfect!" He makes a funny face. "Anyway, she seems to think our top layer problem is communication, and our deeper layer problem is fear."

"Hmm."

"So, she wants us to make a little stage, with a spotlight." He holds up the clamp-on lamp. "She wants us to take turns, under the spotlight, saying what we wish the other one understood about us. And the other one can't talk. They just sit in the dark and watch the show."

"Okay, I guess so." I shrug. I fluff.

"After that, and only after that, questions from the audience will be accepted. The same way it would be with a real performance."

He clamps the lamp onto the bookshelves, plugs it in, and drags a chair under the spotlight. Then he turns off the rest of the lights in the living room. He says, "Do you want to go first?"

"Okay." I sit on the chair, under the spotlight. Dan sits on the sofa, in the dark part of the room. I take a sip of wine. "Okay, what I want to say is just that when I seem to go too much into the past, it's because the present hurts.

I guess I've always been that way but it's only seemed to become much of a problem during times that are the worst for me. Like those years when I wanted a baby so badly and couldn't conceive. And again recently, when I lost my parents, home and business all close together. But the rest of the time, my life's been pretty nice and I wanted to tell you that's largely been because of you. Thank you for that."

I take another sip of wine before continuing. I like this spotlight thing. I said, "I only recently realized my mother did it, too, retreated to the past when the present hurt. And now, so does our daughter. So, when you get mad or mock it or whatever, it hurts, because I'm trying. That's all."

I get off the spotlight chair. Then I say, "Oh, sorry. Did you have any questions? And do you want another glass of wine?" I go for the bottle. I feel kind of overly exposed or something.

Dan says, "I am deeply sorry. I don't know how I could have read everything so wrong and been so mean."

Ugh, this is kind of embarrassing. I say, "Thanks. Here, have some more wine. Your turn!"

Dan takes the stage, bringing his wine with him. I settle in on the couch now, a bit afraid of what I might hear.

He takes a deep breath. He says, "Let me just get to it. Cross-dressing."

After taking an extra big gulp of wine, I nod encouragingly from the shadows.

"The truth is, I've always been drawn to it."

I arrange my face pleasantly. I have read up on this some and am not nearly as horrified with this little chat as I would have been before. When we were young, showing signs of being "different" in that way, was thought to be just the tip of a deep, dark iceberg, one you wouldn't want to explore. We have better information now. During the time Dan's been away, I've changed my mind about all that. Now I feel like it's really no big deal anymore.

I say, "That's okay, hon. Go ahead."

"Okay, so I suppressed it, the best I could. And now, well, in a way I guess I'm saying the same thing you are. I want you to know that I do my best and I want you to accept me. That's it."

I say, "That really is it, isn't it. It seems like things went along one way for many years, and then things changed some, and we both kind of freaked out about it. Fair to say?"

"Fair to say."

We have a long, precious hug under the spotlight, with apologies and kisses, the kind that would make our children groan.

Then I say, "Okay then, let's start over here. How about if I go get some wigs from the shop for you to try on, while you go across the parking lot and get me those chocolates?"

I took our picture later, drunkenly. Our hair, makeup and clothes were done up like twins from the 1970s. The dressing table was littered with candy wrappers and empty wine glasses.

And I don't give a shit what the neighbors would think of it.

Dear Reader,

I hope you enjoyed this collection. It was a lot of fun to write.

A review at your point of purchase would be most appreciated.

Regards,

Carly